BLOOD ON THE SADDLE

BLOOD ON THE SADDLE

by

Lance Howard

Dales Large Print Books
Long Preston, North Yorkshire,
BD23 4ND, England.

British Library Cataloguing in Publication Data.

Howard, Lance
    Blood on the saddle.

A catalogue record of this book is
available from the British Library

ISBN   1-84262-238-2 pbk

First published in Great Britain in 1993 by Robert Hale Limited

Published in Large Print 2003 by arrangement with
Robert Hale Limited

Dales Large Print is an imprint of Library Magna Books Ltd.

Printed and bound in Great Britain by
T.J. (International) Ltd., Cornwall, PL28 8RW

For
Dominique, my parents, Robyn & Steap,
Tannenbaum & Bugsy 'Doodles' Malone.
Also for
Link Hullar, whose encouragement
prompted me to shoot off my first
Peacemaker – though I dang near shot
myself in the foot!

ONE

'I think we'll just take these here supplies on account,' said Brent 'Smiley' Culverin, as he jammed the muzzle of his Colt into the shopkeeper's forehead. Thumbing the hammer back in the prolonged deliberate movement, Brent's lips spread into a cruel smile. The snakelike scar that ran from the right-hand corner of his mouth to his ear – the result of a previous encounter with a lawman in his native Wyoming – gave the expression a hideous aspect, as if the hardcase's grin, half of it at least, ran clean around the side of his head. This peculiar trait had garnered him his nickname, Smiley, one he didn't particularly cotton to, but one with which he was stuck.

Brent watched with perverted joy as the shopkeeper's eyes darted back and forth in their sockets. Sweat beaded on the little 'keep's forehead and dribbled down his pinched features.

Brent's grin widened; he liked it when his threats had the proper effect. In fact, he was known to get downright ugly when they didn't.

'Don't y'all think it's mighty neighbourly of this feller to give us this stuff on the house, boys?' Brent shifted his gaze to the four other men in the shop, all of whom were busy stuffing various goods – jerky, flour, grain and canned goods, as well as matches and various caliber shells – into canvas sacks.

The Culverin brothers looked up in unison, each clucking a dry laugh and flashing exaggerated smiles.

'Sure is, Brent,' said Mace, the next to oldest.

'Downright neighbourly,' Willie, the youngest, echoed.

They returned to the business at hand.

'Well, what do y'all think, Mr Shopkeep?'

Brent's tone carried a jeering quality, one that made the shopkeeper give a violent shudder and flutter his eyelids.

'Y-yes...' he stammered, sweat now streaming freely down his bony wrinkled features. His face had bleached an ashen pallor.

'Even kinder of y'all to crack that ol' safe over yonder.' Brent nudged his head to the left, to the big black safe squatting against the far corner wall. The shopkeep's face drained a shade whiter. 'Course if'n you don't, I'll just have to blow it ... and that would make me downright irritable.' Behind Brent, the Culverin brothers let out chuckles and guffaws.

Beneath his battered, low-slung hat, Brent's eyes narrowed and gleamed like chips of black steel. 'Now move, before I get itchy!'

The shopkeeper gave a rabbit-like nod as Brent pulled the Colt from the man's forehead, leaving a whitened circle indented there. The old man edged around the counter, legs seeming to want to go in two different directions as he crossed the squeaking wooden floorboards to the safe. 'P-please ... d-don't kill me. There ain't much, but you can have it all.' As he kneeled and let his trembling fingers rest on the dial, his face twisted with a pleading look.

'*Please* don't kill me,' Brent mocked, thunking the Colt's barrel against the shopkeeper's temple. The little man winced. A trickle of blood seeped from a quick-forming welt.

'Of course I can have it all!' Brent shouted, making the old man shrink back in fear. 'I'll have anything and everything this cowpoke town has to offer, right boys?' Brent turned his head, watched his brothers give jerky nods. 'Maybe I'll even stay a while, make this town my own. I been lookin' for a place to stow my boots since it got too hot in Cheyenne. Texas can be right easy on a man's hide after a Wyoming winter. What you got for law 'round here, anyhow?' Brent glared at the old man.

'Sheriff Foreman,' the 'keep muttered, eyes darting in his head. 'S-some deputies.'

'How many?'

'Four, five...'

'Nice even number, huh, boys?' Brent laughed, the scar on his face wiggling like a white rattler. The brothers chuckled again. 'Now open it!' Brent thunked the barrel against the old man's temple again, taking care to hit the exact spot he'd banged before.

The little 'keep groaned. His jittery fingers fumbled with the dial, jerking it left then right until the tumblers clicked off the combination. When he was finished, Brent urged him to open the safe with a threatening gesture of his Colt. The shopkeeper grabbed the metal handle and turned it, pulling open the heavy steel door.

'Ah, spit!' Brent cursed, eyeing the meager pouches filled with coin and the sparse bundles of bills, mostly low denomination, he noted with disgust, resting on the safe floor. 'Hardly worth shooting you over, is it?' He gazed at the shopkeeper, a vicious glint flashing from his steel-chip eyes.

The 'keep shook his head, flecks of spit foaming at the edges of his thin lips.

'Boys...'

Brent indicated the safe with a nudge of his Colt. Loomis Culverin straightened and brought over his sack, shoving the old man out of the way and cleaning the contents out of the safe.

The 'keep remained on the floor, his shirt now drenched with sweat.

'Get up!' Brent commanded. The shop-keeper complied, shakily gaining unsteady feet.

'Hey, Brent, come on, we gotta git. Don't matter what this town's got for law, it'll be down on us soon 'nuff if we don't get a move on.' Mace Culverin tied his bag and began to drag it towards the door.

'So?' An expression of contempt flashed across Brent's stubbly features.

'So,' returned Mace, 'if we decide to take this town for later, we'd be better off makin' it more of a surprise attack.'

Brent considered this for a moment. Mace always did have the head of the group. 'Mebbe you're right.'

'What about him?' Loomis put in, indicating the shopkeeper with a jab of his gloved finger. 'If he tells the sheriff, it sure as rain ain't gonna be no surprise.'

The old man's face twisted into a horrified mask. 'N-no, please don't...'

'Shaddup!' Brent snapped, eyes narrowing again. 'Yeah, I see what you mean,' he added in a lower voice. His gaze drilled the shopkeeper, boring in. The old man appeared on the verge of blacking out. 'Turn around!' Brent's tone had turned to ice. 'Slowlike.'

The shopkeeper shuddered, began to turn, barely completing the move before a thunderous shot cracked through the dusty room. The old man seemed to take a giant leap forward, both legs crumbling from under him at the same time. The impact of the slug sent him crashing face first into a shelf stocked with goods. The shelf buckled under the 'keep's weight, collapsed, a shower of canvas packets, jars and canned goods clattering around his dead form. Blood splattered cross the canvas bags and pooled on the dusty floor. The 'keep's body spasmed, then lay still, the back of his head missing.

'Bang...' muttered Brent, squeezing the carved handle of his Colt. He felt a rush of adrenalin surge through his veins, the same fevered tingle he always got when he killed.

The brothers stared, the looks on their faces ones of knowing and muted fear of their oldest brother's inner rage. Then, when Brent turned to them, looking at each in turn, and began to chuckle, they started to laugh with him, nervous laughter that echoed through the solemnness of the deathroom, dying down like ghosts fading.

'Brent, we gotta git,' ventured Mace, a tentative expression flittering across his features, as though he were thinking twice about giving his brother suggestions. He glanced at the body, then back to Brent.

'Yeah.' Brent nodded slowly. The weird half-grin spread over his face again. 'Yeah, let's go.'

The Culverin brothers grabbed their bags, taking up behind Brent as he kicked the door wide. Two passers-by on the boardwalk jumped back as the door banged against the building wall and windows rattled. Brent yelled, 'Yaah!' flashing his Colt. The people scattered, skiddling around the corner of the general store and into the alley.

As the Culverin brothers hauled their sacks to their horses, which were tethered at the rail, the hot Texas sun seared down on them, making sweat, mixed with stirred clouds of dust from their boots, run down their faces in rivulets.

An uproar commenced, the din echoing through the Main Street as townspeople realized what had happened when they saw the Culverins hoist their loot-filled sacks on to their horses.

'C'mon, Brent!' yelled Mace, mounting his roan. 'Let's get outa here!'

Brent leaped on to his horse, grabbing the reins and steadying the animal, who neighed and reared at the din cascading through the street. He scanned the boardwalk, spying a woman with her mouth wide open, shrieking, and levelled his Colt.

A shot spanged in the dirt inches from his horse's front hoof and the animal reared again, causing Brent to jerk the trigger of his own pistol and miss the screaming woman. Though the shot went wide, it came close enough to send her scurrying to the closest shelter.

Brent wrestled his horse under control as another shot, from the same gun, zinged past his ear. Anger ripped through him, sending spasms of hate through his being. He steadied his roan and twisted in his saddle, gaze locking on the cowboy who had taken shots. The outlaw's Colt came up in a blur of motion and his finger squeezed the trigger. The shot seemed lost in the uproar of running, screeching people, but the cowboy, standing by the shop front, flew backwards, jerking off the ground and slamming through a plate-glass window behind him. Shards of glass spiralled, glinting sunlight, to the dust and the cowboy disappeared within the shop.

'Yaah!' Brent yelled, spurring his horse forward. The brothers followed suit, blasting out shots that sent lead plowing through signs and shattering windows. Townspeople raced for cover and the thunder of horses' hooves rumbled through the street. Dust swirled up and, sunlight refracted within, clouded the street with a thick yellowish haze, as the Culverins disappeared over the town's horizon.

'What in tarnation's all the ruckus about?' blurted Sheriff Frank Foreman, springing to his feet as the front door of his office burst open. Abraham Lincoln Hullar, the sheriff's plump specimen of a deputy, stood framed in the doorway, gulping deep breaths of air. He swabbed his dripping features with a dirty red bandanna. His cherubic face sported a flustered expression that made his eyes appear set back in his head farther than seemed humanly possible. His normally ruddy complexion was blanched.

By the time the deputy managed to put a coherent sentence together, Sheriff Foreman had already grabbed his Stetson, checked the chambers of his Smith & Wesson and crossed the room.

'Well, speak up, speak up!' urged Sheriff Foreman. 'Half the gall-darned town must be shoutin' in the street. Somethin' mighty big's gotta be up!' Sheriff Foreman peered at the deputy, who couldn't have topped five-feet-five and had a paunch that strained the belt-line of his brown shirt. Taking another deep breath, the deputy struggled to bring himself under control.

'Men – outlaws – just shot up old Silas at the general store somethin' awful! Heared to tell it was the Culverin brothers.'

'Oh, lordy!' Sheriff Foreman blew out a long sigh and shook his head. 'I was afraid them boys would find their way to these parts sooner or later. They've left a trail from Wyoming to West Texas as bloody as anything I've seen in my fifty years. Well, I got no choice; I gotta bring 'em in. What else did they do?'

'Put one in Lucus Havelin, but he'll make it. Most of the rest is property damage and a lot of scare in the locals.'

Foreman ran a hand through his greying beard; the hand carried a slight tremble. He knew the Culverins' reputation, knew the bloodshed they were responsible for. Many a lawman and local sheriff had sought to bring them down, always ending up on the lead end of Brent Culverin's Colt. Given a choice, Foreman thought he'd have preferred dealing with the James boys; their reputations were nearly the same. Foreman had grave doubts about living to tell about it if he went after the outlaws, but he didn't see any other choice. He was the law in Matadero and it was his duty.

Sheriff Foreman had four part-time deputies besides Abe Hullar, all of whom were pretty handy with a six-shooter. Abe? Well, the squat lawman wasn't a bad shot, but sometimes he had trouble getting out of his own way. It would be six to four in the sheriff's favor manwise, but that fact provided him with scant comfort.

'Get over to the Cazador and roust Parker, Jonas, Stevens and Matino from their poker game. Tell them to mount up and be prepared to track down the Culverins...'

'And?' asked Deputy Hullar, as if catching the sheriff's hesitation. He wrung his hands, face tense but determined.

'Tell them to make sure to say goodbye to their loved ones.' The sheriff pressed his lips together.

Abe's Adam's apple bobbed downward, then jerked up again.

Foreman stepped past the deputy, pausing at the door. 'I'm gonna settle things down a bit. Tell them to be ready to ride in an hour in front of the Cazador. And Abe, if y'all want to back out, now's the time.' He peered at his deputy, never for an instant

22

doubting the man's courage, but knowing if any of them had a chance of coming back in one piece, Abe was the least likely to. Foreman hoped giving Abe an out would absolve himself of some of the guilt he knew he'd feel if he survived a shootout and Abe didn't.

'No, I'm a'goin',' Hullar said, resolve in his tone. 'I knowed someday it might come to this and I ain't about to pull out now that it has.'

'You're a good man, Abe. If I never told you that, I'm tellin' you now.' With that, Sheriff Foreman stepped through the doorway.

An hour later, six men – Sheriff Foreman, Deputy Abraham Lincoln Hullar and four deputies – sat on their horses in front the El Cazador Saloon. Each face showed a strained tightness, each body a rigidness that made obvious his feelings about hunting down the Culverin brothers. Sheriff Foreman had managed to get the townspeople calmed –

most of them had gone back to their business, calmly making their way along the street to their particular destination. He had viewed the carnage at the general store. He felt bile rise in his throat as he thought about the sight of the slain old man, and felt anger course through his veins at the utter senselessness of the loss of life. The store had been closed and its doors boarded over by two of Silas's workers. Foreman vowed that if he didn't get to take the Culverins in, he would at least make sure one of them tasted lead from his Smith & Wesson.

'I ain't gonna try foolin' ya, men,' the sheriff said in an even tone. 'These hardcases are as bad as they come. There ain't much likelihood all of us will make it back livin'. If you spot one of the sidewinders, don't stop to ask questions or advice from me: shoot to kill. I want something to show Silas's widow. Understood?' He glanced at each man in turn, who nodded his understanding. He saw fear in their eyes, but along with it the resolve and raw courage that fashioned these men of the West.

'They got a little over an hour's start on us,' the sheriff continued. 'They headed south and there's only one town within a day's ride of here. They gotta be headin' that way. Cain't see them passin' it up. Let's go!' Sheriff Foreman kicked up his horse into motion and its beating hooves threw up cyclones of dust as he drove it into full gallop. The deputies followed, a beat behind.

Three miles on, the sheriff brought his bay to a stop. Mopping sweat from his brow then replacing the Stetson, he dismounted, sharp eyes scanning the ground.

'What is it?' questioned Abe, looking intently at the sheriff.

Foreman kneeled, scooping up a handful of something from the hard-packed trail. 'One of 'em leakin' feed. His bag musta sprung a leak or Lucus got off a lucky shot when he took aim on Brent Culverin. Funny they haven't noticed it...'

He glanced at Abe, who shrugged, the

inference seemingly lost on him. Foreman turned his head back and studied the grain cupped in his hand, then gazed at the thick line of it leading down the trail like gunpowder. Odd, he thought, that the sack hadn't run dry by now. He had noticed the stuff nearly a mile and half back. Straightening, he climbed back on his horse and peered at the trail. It wound through a ravine about a mile ahead, its sides cluttered with thick clumps of manzanita and scraggly short trees, as well as clusters of rock and scattered boulders. Its side sloped sharply, and, at places, rose up on either side sheer as buildings. Something about the whole scene bothered him, but he couldn't pin it down.

Turning to the other man he said, 'Look, I got a funny feelin' about this. I don't know what it is exactly, but let's go forward a bit more cautiouslike.'

He scooted his horse into a canter, keeping a wary eye trained to either side, as well as ahead. The road began to twist at peculiar angles, snaking through thicker scrub, drifting sand and strewn rock. Still the grain trail led onward, in a pattern almost too perfect. By now he was sure it was being set purposely, leading them into something. A ball of apprehension swelled in his gut and made him want to turn around and ride back to Matadero.

To either side, the ravine began to rise at sloping angles, higher and more steep with each hundred feet they covered. Boulders of various sizes piled at odd-spaced intervals. The grain trail led on. The ball of fear in Sheriff Foreman's belly grew larger and he slowed his horse, scanning the surroundings suspiciously.

'I'm a'gettin' the same feelin',' he heard Abe say beside him. Turning, Foreman saw the tension etched on the deputy's ruddy face.

'Something's wrong, deadly wrong.' Foreman's voice came in a cold tone. 'This grain shoulda run out by now, or at least one of 'em would have noticed. They ain't survived this long without at least some smarts.'

'A trap?' Abe's eyes had a nervous dart.

Foreman nodded. 'Any of you know a better way towards Raco, other than through this here ravine?' The men shook their heads.

'Not 'less you want to go an extra day around, through the scorpions and rattlers,' said Abe, frowning. 'By the time we get there that way, they'd have done the same thing in Raco as they did in Matadero and we'd lose our chance.'

'Doesn't look like we've got a whole lot of choice, then, does it. Keep a–'

A high-pitched whine shrieked past Sheriff Foreman's ear, nearly taking a piece off his lobe. A cold chill shuddered down his spine, despite the heat. He knew the sound of a bullet when he heard it, and knew this one had just come too darned close.

'They're here!' he shouted, as his horse reared, neighing. He fought to get the animal under control. A volley of shots sounded, echoing like thunder from the ravine walls. Clumps of dirt gouged from the road as lead burrowed in. A slug tore through one of the deputies, knocking him from his horse. The horse bolted and the deputy groaned and quivered on the ground. Foreman managed to bring his horse to calm and leaped off with agility surprising for his age. He doubled over and went to the wounded man, unholstering his Smith & Wesson and firing protective shots at the same time. He wasn't positive where the shots were coming from, just the general direction. He hoped the return fire would give him enough time to get the injured man to safety.

Heaving the deputy up with his free arm, Foreman hurled the man toward a line of waist-high boulders. Lead spanged from rock, ricocheting, chipping off shards of stone. Foreman got the man down behind the rock, then turned to get a bead on the bushwhackers.

The other deputies had managed to find protective spots, hidden behind the manzanita clumps or low trees. Even Abe made it to shelter, looking less conspicuous behind a clump of brush than Foreman would have thought.

Their horses, he saw, had turned around and were galloping back towards town, so the sheriff knew even if they got out of this, which didn't look likely at the moment, that would be a minor problem. He counted himself lucky the Culverins hadn't managed to kill them all with the surprise attack. Perhaps they hadn't wanted to, at least not right away. He guessed the outlaws were the kind of snakes who liked to play with their prey before devouring it. Foreman reloaded then glanced at the deputy lying beside him, groaning. A splotch of crimson welled on the man's shirt. It didn't look good and would get a whole lot worse if they didn't end this soon and get the man some medical attention.

A hush fell over the surroundings as the gunfire lulled. He guessed they were reloading.

Sheriff Foreman used the opportunity. He scrambled from behind the boulder, pumping off shots in the general direction of the outlaws, and scooted over to Abe.

'Any location on them?' he asked the deputy. He had been too busy with the wounded man and hoped Hullar had managed to spot where the gunfire had come from.

Hullar spat. 'See that slope up towards the left yonder?'

Foreman nodded.

'Some coming from behind the rocks there. More farther on over to the south of 'em – why didn't they just kill us?'

'They wanted to make a game of it, I'm bettin'.' Foreman looked thoughtful. 'Might have been a mistake on their part.'

'Let's hope so.' Hullar let out the breath he was holding.

'Why don't we see if we can't sidewind 'em, smoke 'em out into the open where we can get a clean shot. Cover me while I get to the others.'

Abe nodded, then jumped up and began blasting shots towards the boulders. Sheriff Foreman darted forward, towards the next deputy. Bullets whistled around him, plowing up dirt inches from his running feet. A slug seared the back of his leg, throwing off his dash and sending him diving for cover. A scarlet gash showed through his ripped trousers. He winced, clenching his teeth against the pain, but he knew the wound wasn't serious. He fired six shots in return, the feel of his kicking pistol comforting his grip, then hastily reloaded. Working his way to the other deputies, using more caution this time, he told them the plan. They in turn began positioning themselves along the hill, in an effort to surround the Culverins.

Sheriff Foreman, moving to another spot, caught sight of the gang, recognizing the leader, Brent, from the snaky scar on his face and from a poster he had seen of the outlaw. The hardcase had secured himself between some brush and a boulder, but not effectively enough. The sheriff guessed it was probably a sense of bravado that motivated the outlaw, making him a little less cautious than he should have been. The outlaw leader was grinning his weird half-grin, drawing a level on the plump and now partially exposed form of Abe Hullar.

'That's what you get for being over-confident from winnin' all the time,' Foreman mumbled. His Smith & Wesson flashed up. He jerked off a shot, barely aimed. The outlaw recoiled, a spurt of scarlet splashing the rock in front of him before he could clamp a hand over a shoulder wound. The hardcase fell back, scurrying along the ground to better cover behind the boulder and Foreman bleated a satisfied whoop. 'That'll teach the varmint!'

Then all hell broke loose!

The other brothers, upon seeing their leader taken down, scurried from cover, carelessly scrambling down the hill, their guns flying off shots. The sheriff ducked as lead spanged all around him.

The deputies fired at the suddenly mobile targets, missing. One of the brothers blasted off a shot and a deputy bounded backward from a tree bole, crashing down into the dirt. He lay still and Sheriff Foreman felt a knife of regret twist his belly.

Sheriff Foreman yelled, 'Let 'em have it, men!' and the deputies began to fire round after round. The air filled with the whine of lead, the smell of gunpowder and the tramping of boots. Shots thundered through the ravine in a deafening volley. The sheriff felt a glimmer of elation spark in his gut as he saw the Culverin gang scramble around a bend in the hillside.

They were retreating!

With their leader down, the rest had lost their nerve; outlaws were mostly cowards at heart in Foreman's opinion.

The sheriff trotted forward, still firing sporadic shots; he couldn't be too careful, he reckoned. His deputies followed heading for the boulder where Brent Culverin had fallen.

Sheriff Foreman waved off the gunfire. Listening intently, he caught the sound of hooves fading into the distance.

'Should we go after 'em?' one of the men asked.

'No, we got one, the leader. Unless I miss my guess, they'll either disband because they ain't got no real guts or...' The sheriff let his words trail off.

'They'll come after him,' put in Abe in a meek tone.

There was still the matter of 'him', thought Foreman. Nearing the boulder, he slowed his pace, knowing most outlaws, even if seriously wounded, would squeeze off a last shot with dying fingers if given the opportunity. He held up a halting hand to the deputies as he cautiously rounded the boulder, gun advanced, finger tense on the trigger.

The effort proved unnecessary, he discovered. Brent Culverin lay in the dust, unmoving, his Colt lying a few feet away. A scarlet patch soaked his shirt, but Foreman could tell the leader was still breathing. Too bad. He nudged the outlaw with a boot toe, peering at the scarred face.

'Ugly *hombre*,' said Abe, shuddering.

Foreman agreed. He walked off, scouting the area until he located a lone horse tethered to a tree. On the roan lay a sack, a knife-slit bleeding grain, plus two empties, confirming his earlier suspicions. He led the horse over to the boulder, planning on using it to carry his wounded deputy.

A sudden movement stopped him short. One of the deputies had been leaning over Brent Culverin and the gang leader had exploded into action. Foreman cursed himself for letting the relief of the moment make him let his guard down and make a stupid mistake. He should have thought Culverin might be playing possum, but he hadn't figured anyone could lie that still with a bullet lodged in his shoulder.

An odd-looking gun flashed into Culverin's hand, pulled from beneath the outlaw's duster. The deputy pounced but the hardcase triggered a shot. The deputy flew backwards, a bloodless hole between his eyes. Foreman darted forward, Smith & Wesson threatening. 'Drop it! Or I swear I'll put an extra hole in your ugly head!'

The gang leader hesitated, as if thinking over his chances, then let the odd weapon slide from his fingers. Abe rushed up and grabbed it, examining it, then handing the revolver to the sheriff.

'Weird lookin' critter,' said Abe.

'A .32,' mumbled the sheriff, turning the stubby weapon over his hand. 'A Reid's Knuckleduster. Usually a back-up weapon; can also be used as a bludgeon.' Peering at it, the sheriff saw its lack of barrel, bullets firing directly from the revolver chamber, and its hammerlike handle. The thought of such a little piece being so deadly made him shiver.

Pocketing the weapon, he added, 'There's some rope holding the supplies to the sidewinder's horse. Tie him up and make sure he don't pull no more surprises.'

'You'll regret this...' Brent Culverin said through clenched teeth. He drilled the sheriff with his black-steel gaze. 'That's a promise.'

'I already do.' Foreman turned away as the other deputies covered the leader. He went to the fallen man hit by the .32, bent and examined him. A sick feeling crawled through his belly.

Straightening, he made his way to the other downed men. One, whom he had known was dead right off, lay sprawled in the dirt near the tree. A brief look told him he was right. He knew the man's wife and dreaded being the one who would have to tell her about her husband's death, but he knew it was a necessary, if gut-wrenching part of his job.

Making his way to the other man, he saw this one was still breathing and yelled for a deputy to bring the horse over. This man stood a chance at life – if they got him to the doc soon. He had Abe and the remaining deputy help him secure the wounded man to the leader's roan, all the while keeping a watchful eye on the outlaw. It was at least five miles into town; with the heat, it was going to feel like ten.

Brent Culverin glanced at the wounded man then at the sheriff, his dark eyes narrowed into slits. The weird half-grin on his face lengthened.

'I'd just as soon put a bullet in you here and now, Culverin. Just give me a reason.' Foreman shoved the outlaw forward – the leader's hands were laced behind his back, but his feet had been left free for walking.

'You'll never be able to hold me, Sheriff. Ain't no jail strong enough to keep a Culverin for long.'

Foreman didn't answer. As they trudged towards Matadero, the sheriff's feelings were mixed, the satisfaction of bringing in one of the most notorious gunmen the West had known muted by the grim sense of dread loss at the death of two good men.

He wondered if it were worth it.

TWO

Sheriff Frank Foreman ran a hand through his grey-sprinkled beard and leaned back in his overstuffed chair, swinging his booted feet on to the desk. He gazed a moment into the flame from the kerosene wall lamp, lost in thought and the vague feeling of doom that had come over him shortly after downing the bowl of stew Abe had brought him from the El Cazador an hour ago. He'd swigged a generous gulp of whiskey from the flask tucked away in his desk, but the feeling had refused to leave him.

Three days had passed since he'd brought in Brent Culverin, and in those three days time had seemed to drag like a steamy West Texas night. He'd done his duty informing the deceased deputies' widows of their husbands' bravery in chasing down the outlaws, but it had settled in his belly like bad whiskey. In his mind, he still saw the tears streaming down their faces. The wounded deputy would live, though he wouldn't have much use in one arm. They'd gotten him to the doc just in time. Abe had escaped without even a scratch. Who'd a thought it, Sheriff Foreman mused. What the Good Lord hadn't given Hullar in swiftness He'd made up for in luck. Foreman was thankful for that.

Still that feeling of dread plagued him. Brent Culverin lay stretched out on the rickety cot in one of the office's two jail cells; the other cell was empty. Foreman shot the hardcase a glance and the dread feeling worked its way deeper into his soul. In his heart, he knew there was scant chance the Culverin brothers would disband and let the whole thing drop. He'd only told that to the deputies to ease their minds. Inside he knew better. Although he had seen outlaw bands fall apart after losing their leader, he knew the Culverins were among the worst bandits in the West; they weren't about to let their leader go to trial and face a hangman's noose. But why hadn't they struck before now? What were they waiting for? Foreman reckoned it was probably another one of their cat and mouse games.

Sheriff Foreman swung his feet off the desk and unholstered his Smith & Wesson, checking the cylinders, then reholstering it. Pushing himself up, he strode over to the coffee pot and poured himself a lukewarm tin cupful. He took a couple of deep gulps, then, facing the cell, eyed Brent Culverin. Foreman had made his decision: He was determined that if the Culverins did intend to strike, they would not get what they came for.

'You'll hang in the morning,' Foreman said with no emotion. He saw Brent's head turn towards him, saw the leader's grotesque grin lengthen. In the dusky amber glow of the kerosene lamp, the scar seemed alive, darting like a scorpion's tail. It made Foreman want to take a backward step, avert his eyes, but he forced himself to hold his ground.

Keeping his voice steady he said, 'I said you'll hang in the morning. I don't see nothin' too funny 'bout that.'

Brent uttered a short contempt-filled laugh. 'Yeah? Is that the way the law works in Texas, now?' His black-steel eyes narrowed, boring into the sheriff's own blue ones.

'That's the way it works in my town. You're too dangerous to let go for long. I ain't never been one to take unnecessary chances. The reward on you boys says dead or alive. You killed old Silas and two of my deputies; that's all the convictin' I need.'

'I said you'd regret the day you took me in; I'm sayin' it again. You got one chance, Sheriff. Open this here cell door and maybe I'll let you live.'

Something in the outlaw's tone made the sheriff half consider reaching for the keys and swinging the door wide, as if Brent Culverin had exerted some sort of evil spell that extended across the room and gripped him. No, he wouldn't let the hardcase intimidate him.

'That's about as likely for me to do as it is for you to take up church-goin'.' The sheriff frowned, lips tight.

Culverin laughed, an evil sound, and turned his head to stare up at the ceiling. 'Nice knowin' ya, Sheriff,' he muttered through clenched teeth.

Foreman felt frozen in place for an instant, then managed to shake off some of his worry. Turning, he walked back towards his desk, stopping short as a sound filtered in from the darkened street. He started despite himself, splashing coffee on to the desk. Making his way over to the window, he peered out into the blue-black shadows covering the main street. Scanning it, he was unable to pinpoint the source of the noise, which had sounded to him like the whoop of an Indian. As he started back to the desk, he noticed Brent Culverin had turned towards him again, the half-grin on his stubbly face.

'Shoulda taken my offer, Sheriff. Too late, now.'

Foreman slid his fingers over the butt of his gun. 'I should just put one right between your eyes and be done with it–'

The door burst open with a thunderous *crack!* rattling as it careened into the wall, partially torn from its hinges. The sheriff whirled, hand whipping back to the Smith & Wesson, but unable to pull it free before four men, the lower half of their faces covered by bandannas, flooded into the office.

'Don't!' one of them yelled, gesturing menacingly with a Colt. 'Just step on back a bit and start sayin' whatever prayer suits you.'

The sheriff complied, as the men came farther into the room and closed the door.

'Now, real slowlike, reach down and unbuckle your gunbelt – that's right, nice and easy.'

The sheriff unfastened the buckle, letting the belt thunk to the floor. His heart pounded in his throat and he knew as sure as he was going to die he should have hanged Brent Culverin the day he brought him in.

One of the outlaws grabbed the key-ring and set about extricating Brent Culverin, whose eyes glinted with vicious lights as he glared at the sheriff. The outlaw leader went to the desk, locating his Colt and Knuckle-duster, plus the flask of whiskey. Unscrewing the cap, he swigged half the contents and wiped a hand across his mouth.

'You know, Sheriff,' he said in a measured voice while checking his Colt, 'sometimes I can be a downright tolerant man...'

He looked up. 'This ain't one of the times. Say *adios, amigo*...'

The hardcase jerked up his Colt and triggered. A shot blasted. A blooming scarlet rose suddenly appeared on Sheriff Fore-man's shirt as he took an involuntary leap backward, slamming into the rickety wooden table that held the coffee pot. The table buckled. The sheriff crashed down after it, sprawled. A snake of blood slithered from the corner of his mouth into his beard.

The Culverin brothers tore the bandannas from their faces.

'What in Hades took y'all so long?' Brent shouted at Mace, who recoiled. 'Any longer an' I'd been swingin' from a danged noose!'

Mace shrugged. 'We needed a plan.'

'You call this a plan? I thought you had a head on your shoulders. If it ever happens again you better danged well think a mite faster – or that head of your'n will have itself an extra hole!' Brent's hard eyes drilled Mace and Mace took a backward step.

'We'd better git,' Mace offered hesitantly.

Opening the door, the gang moved out, sidling down the boardwalk and around the building into an alley where five horses were hitched.

'We paid the livery a visit and got your horse back before comin' here,' said Mace, mounting. 'The stable feller was real polite until we killed him!' Mace chuckled at his own joke, but Brent didn't seem to find it very funny.

'I want this town, boys,' he said, glaring at them. 'I want 'em to know the penalty for messin' with Brent Culverin.' With a whoop he kicked his roan into motion, the others following. They tore around the corner, guns drawn, muzzles blasting flame. Windows shattered and boards splintered under the volley of hot lead.

Men, rousted by the din, began pouring from the saloon. A bandaged Lucus Havelin and the remaining deputy drew pistols and returned fire, each diving for meager cover behind barrels.

Brent drew a bead on one, fired. The deputy jumped up, winged, exposing himself to Brent's line of fire. Brent blasted four rapid shots, riddling the man, who collapsed.

The other man, Lucus, pumped lead at the horse-bound figure, missing in his haste. Slugs tore into the barrel protecting him. One plowed through the other side, an inch from his head. He flung himself for better cover, but was too slow. Mace filled him full of lead before the man even made it three feet. Lucus tumbled off the boardwalk into the street and lay still.

Two of the brothers lassoed a supporting beam and shot forward on their horses. The beam groaned, whined, snapped, its brittle wood no match for the horses' power. The roof overhang crashed to the boardwalk, splintering. The brothers guffawed, whooped, hollered.

Brent guided his horse up beside the others, shouting, 'We got a deputy and the sheriff. The other deputy lived, I heard Foreman say so. He's over to the doc's. See that he don't make it through the next hour. And find that little fat *hombre* and show 'im the same courtesy!'

Mace and Loomis split up to tend to their tasks. Luke and Willie followed Brent as he fashioned the town to his liking ...

Jake Donovan sidled up to the polished wooden bar in the Sawdust saloon in

Wishingstar, Texas, planting his denims on to the stool and ordering a bourbon. The bartender, Wayland Earls, grinned and slapped a glass on the counter, filling it. Jake set his Stetson on the next stool and wiped his brow, shooting a glance at the roulette tables, then the stage that during the evening hours sported dancing girls. The Sawdust was one of the biggest saloons in Wishingstar, with the most amenities, but Jake still preferred the small cowpoke drinkeries he had frequented in the past. He reckoned he had never been much for the big city, if you could rightly call Wishingstar the big city. Still, it was larger by a darnsight than Matadero, where he originally hailed from.

'How long you stayin', Jake?' asked Wayland, eyeing him with a knowing look. The barkeep's lips parted a fraction, revealing brown-stained teeth.

'Never know.' Jake shrugged and sipped bourbon. 'What makes you ask?' Jake sensed something was up with the wiry barkeep.

Jake had been in Wishingstar for only a couple of months, but he had struck up an odd sort of friendship with the 'tender. He was straightforward and Jake liked that.

'Well, jest think the need for hired guns is gettin' less and less, is all. Thought you might be lookin' at headin' home, now that the West is tamin'.'

'Taming? You could have fooled me! And as for going to Matadero ... I doubt it. It's been fifteen years; I think I've got it out of my system by now.'

'You ain't foolin' nobody, Mr Donovan, least of all yerself. I know you been hankerin' to stop your driftin' and git home.'

'How do you come by that, oh wise and wonderous one?' asked Jake, imitating the fake gypsy Wayland sometimes brought in for the evening crowd.

'You don't get to be barkeep twenty years without pickin' up some sort of handle on human nature. And from what you told me of your southward trail over the past year, you been inchin' closer and closer to Matadero.'

Jake shook his head, a little too forcefully. 'Matadero was a long time ago ... I got no desire to go back so you can safely put away your crystal ball.'

'Uh-huh. Well, here's somethin' that jest might change your tune – you got no more obstacles, now.'

'What does that mean?' Curiosity mixed with surprise rose in Jake's mind.

'Jest that old Diego Cardona up and died a few days back – last of the Cardona clan, I hear tell.'

Jake stiffened, feeling as if a cold Montana wind had just blown through him. He hadn't heard the Cardona name in years, but had thought it only weeks ago. Jake felt his mind start to wander back to that time, to the dusty streets of Matadero and a woman who could still turn up a powerful feeling in his soul.

'Well?' prodded Wayland, breaking Jake from his thoughts.

'Well, what?' Jake shot back, tone more than a little defensive.

'Well, you'll be packin' for the south in the mornin', I bet, won't you? I mean with the old man out of the way...'

'How'd you know about that? And why are you so all-fired eager to get rid of me?' Jake cocked an eyebrow.

'Like I said, in twenty years you pick up things. And it ain't that I'm so all-fired eager, neither! It's jest that I know personal pain when I see it and you, *amigo*, got a heap.'

'You're wastin' yourself being a barkeep, Wayland. They pay them fancy doctors in Boston a lot more money to do what you do.'

'Yeah, but would I give up all this here luxury, I ask you – oh-oh...'

The thumbing back of a hammer and the chill metal pressure of a gun muzzle on his neck made Jake's blood run cold. As the gun pressed deeper into his flesh, he cursed himself for being too immersed in his own thoughts and past feelings to detect the person sneaking up and getting the drop on him. Usually he didn't make such mistakes, and this one might just be his last.

'Jake Donovan...'

A young, hard-edged voice spoke behind him. The voice, its barely detectable quiver and the way in which the man had said his name, told Donovan what was up. He glanced at Wayland, whose face had become a taut mask. Obviously the barkeep hadn't been paying attention either.

'Can I turn around?' Jake asked, keeping his voice steady. He weighed the likelihood of getting his Peacemaker .45 out of its holster and plugging the stranger before taking a bullet through the neck, quickly deciding the odds weren't in his favor.

'Real slow – and no sudden moves,' the voice commanded. 'And get your hands up!'

Jake complied, raising his hands and manoeuvring himself around on the stool. He turned to stare into the face of a young cowboy – no more than twenty-five or twenty-six, Jake would have guessed – levelling a Colt at Jake's chest. He couldn't place ever having seen the boy before, but he knew it was merely a different face on the same specter that constantly haunted him.

The young cowboy, fighting a nervous twitch at his eye, began to speak. 'They call you *El Vengador* – the Avenger from Matadero. I heard it told you even outdrew a Cardona once, and things been hot for you ever since. But you're gettin' old and slow; I got the up on you easy.' A proud look spread over the man's tense features. Jake studied the cowboy, seeing the rigid set of his body, the white fingers clamped too tightly on the Colt's handle. That made him nervous. One wrong move and he knew the boy would trigger a shot from pure reflex.

'I don't know if you'd call forty all that old, son, and as for slow, well, let's hope you don't have to find out.' Jake frowned. 'Stupid might apply in this case, though. It'll remind me to be more careful in the future.'

'There ain't no future, Mr Avenger, leastwise not for you. I been scoutin' you for a month, now, thinkin' how much respect I'd have in this town if'n I outdrew the mighty Jake Donovan.'

Something in Jake's belly sank when he heard the boy say it outright. Now that he thought about it, he had noticed the youth observing him every now and then, but had thought nothing of it at the time. Maybe the kid was right: he was getting old and slow. One thing for sure: he was sure getting a powerful urge to just hide from his past and live a normal life. This just brought it home to him. This boy was one in a long series of challenges all gunnies seemed disposed to facing, another nameless brave trying to earn his feathers. Jake had no wish to fight the boy; he knew the results. He had let himself be drawn into it once before and that was enough. Usually he was better at avoiding the situation.

All that didn't matter a lick, now. He had to think of something fast.

'Now, look, why don't you just put your gun away and sit and have a drink with me, son? We don't have to let this get out of hand. I concede; you're the better man, you win, you got your stripes–'

'Don't mock me, Donovan!' The youth's face splashed crimson with rage. 'I came here to get myself a reputation and I don't aim to leave without it!'

'I told you, you got your reputation. You faced me and I backed down. Let that be enough.' Jake felt his own temper boil. Even if he got out of this, he knew the cowboy's own pigheadedness would put him in a pine box soon enough. Jake hated himself for getting into this position but he had a ray of hope. He saw Wayland beginning to ease along the bar. The youth seemed too intent on Jake to notice. Jake caught the barkeep's movement from the corner of his eye, but took care not to let it show.

'No, I gotta outdraw you!' the boy snapped, face gone from crimson to purple. 'That's the way of the West!'

'The way of the West is changin', son. Go with it. You'll be better off. Elsewise you'll wind up on the short end of that shooter someday. Ain't nobody that can avoid it, believe me. Take it from someone who knows; ain't nothin' but lonely times and sorrow being a hired gun. Nothing but empty feelings.' Jake drilled the cowboy with his gaze, keeping his attention while Wayland edged another few steps.

'You're wrong! You only want to keep the fame for yourself!' The youth was shouting and Jake knew he had to be careful; if he got the cowboy too riled, the Colt would go off.

Wayland had managed to slide around the end of the counter and work his way between two tables to a position diagonally behind the youth. Jake fought to keep the boy's attention focused on him; it was crucial, now.

'OK, look, if you have to do this fine. But not in here. We'll meet in the street and it will be fair.' Jake indicated the batwing doors with a finger.

Excitement jumped into the boy's eyes. Jake had seen that look before – too often; it was the look that usually preceded the death-stare.

The cowboy waved his Colt and Jake slid off the stool, careful to turn the boy towards the doors and not into a position where he could see Wayland. Wayland had grabbed a sawed-off from beneath the bar and had it poised butt first about shoulder level, obviously intending to knock the boy senseless and leave him with nothing more than a headache. The 'keep had moved within three feet of the youth.

'No!' blurted the boy, spinning. Jake cursed, realizing he must have made some inadvertent signal with his gaze, pinpointing Wayland's approach. The boy, fevered as he was, had caught it. The youth's Colt swung in a short arc towards the barkeep.

Jake lunged, thrusting an arm under the youth's elbow and jerking up. The boy's finger squeezed the trigger, but the sharp upward movement of his arm caused the shot to go wild. The slug plowed into the chandelier, which shattered in an explosion of glass. Shards rained to the floor.

Wayland leaped sideways and Jake snapped a fist into the youth's jaw. A heavy crack sounded as knuckle slammed bone. The boy's lower face took on a distorted shape. His eyes rolled back and his Colt dropped from nerveless fingers. He crumbled to the floor, senseless.

'Sorry, 'bout that, Jake,' said Wayland. 'Guess my sneakin' days are long past me.'

Jake flashed a nervous grin. 'Don't be sorry ... you just saved this boy's life – and mine!'

'I'll get the sheriff to come pick him up. A night in a cell ought to cool him off some.'

'Doesn't matter.' Jake's voice held resignation. 'He'd just get the notion to try it again. I've seen it too many times before.'

'What are you gonna do?' Wayland moved back around the bar and stowed the sawed-off.

Jake went to the bar, plucked his Stetson

from the counter and put it on. He glanced over his shoulder at the unconscious cowboy, then back to Wayland. 'Looks like Billy the Kid here just made up my mind for me.' The 'keep poured him another bourbon and Jake drank it down.

'You're goin' back?'

'Looks that way. I don't reckon I'll ever be able to escape the past, but with Cardona gone maybe it'll at least let me be.' He gazed at Wayland, spreading his hands. 'But who knows? Maybe my rambling spirit can't be happy in one place anymore.'

Jake brought his horse to a stop at the crest of the sloping trail that snaked into Matadero. In the distance, he saw the little town, its rambling wooden structures spread across the scrabbly patch of countryside. It wasn't pretty as far as Texas towns went, but he had been born and reared there and it still sent a tingle of old feelings and images through the memory. Fifteen long and hard years had passed since he rode away, never intending to return, never intending to even lay sight on its dusty streets again. Never intending to see...

Well, he couldn't dwell on her, now. That was too long ago and things were surely different. She had probably married and settled down with some wealthy rancher; she was worthy of that, certainly more worthy than of a rambler such as himself. She deserved far better than he could have ever offered, and events had made their separation inevitable, at least to his mind. Cardona had owned the town then, but, now, with the old man gone, who knew what the sun-battered streets held?

'Well, Zach,' he mumbled, slapping his horse's neck playfully. 'Whatta you think? Think there's any kind of life there for your old buddy, Jake? Or do you think we've been on the road too long to call any place home?'

The bay whinnied, as if in response. Jake wondered sometimes if the animal weren't capable of understanding human speech.

Well, at least they seemed to understand each other, knew the drive to roam and outrun the past. But now the past was facing him. He might have run from it before, but now there was no turning back. Some ghosts, he reckoned, just had to be confronted. Maybe those ghosts would destroy him this time, or raise the shade of the coward he sometimes suspected he had become.

Matadero had a way of testing a man's mettle.

Jake gave Zach a gentle nudge and the bay cantered forward. He felt his nerves resist as they approached, but he fought the apprehension down. For an instant, he struggled with another memory, one of the woman he had left behind. He couldn't deny the old feelings – some comfortable, some not – swelling within him. What if he did see her again? Would he feel things he once felt? Would rage grip him if he saw her in the arms of another man? She certainly had every right to be.

'Women like Nellie Cantrell don't wait around for the likes of men like me...' he muttered to Zach. 'They got more breedin' than that.'

A little voice inside him hoped he was wrong.

Jake approached the outskirts of Matadero, a torrent of familiarity surging over him and making his legs feel weak. He gazed upon the buildings, the Costanza Hotel on the north edge, a tonsorial parlor – that was new, he realized – an eatery, bank, the El Cazador saloon – this place brought a rush of warm feeling into his being; he remembered spending many a night there – and a boarded-up general store.

Something hit him. At first he couldn't be sure what it was, then it started to come to him. First, the shop *was* boarded up. Why? He s'posed it wasn't all that unusual in itself, but something looked – no, *felt* – wrong. He began noticing other things, small things, such as boarded-over windows here and there, a missing part of a roof, and a peculiar absence of townsfolk on the streets. Matarado used to bustle with activity at this time of day, near noon. If anything, the town should have grown since he left, not turned into a ghost town. The few people he did spot cast him nervous glances and scurried on their way. Why were they so skittish? The town used to welcome strangers with open arms.

Jake shook his head, not liking the feeling that had come over him.

Far in the distance he could see the bulky shape of the Cardona Mansion, looking like a sentry standing guard over the town. The sentry seemed oddly unarmed, now, and for that he was just as glad. But he didn't explain the way this town was acting; Cardona's passing should have been a relief to the people.

'What's up here, Zach?' he asked the bay. The horse didn't answer, but Jake could tell by its slightly stiffer gait the animal sensed the same thing he did.

Slowing the horse as he neared the saloon,

Jake gave the street a final survey. Yes, there was tension here; he felt it thick as desert dust. Jake sat his horse in front of the El Cazador, patting Zach's neck gently and making sure his Winchester 30-30 was still secure in its saddle boot. If there were a threat, Jake would be ready for it.

Pushing through the batwing doors, Jake saw the interior of the saloon hadn't changed much. The big gilded mirror still hung on the wall behind the bar; bottles stocked with liquor lined the shelves; a dozen or so tables spotted the big room; the ugly patterned wallpaper still covered the walls; and a long winding staircase still led to the upper rooms. He felt the familiar grinding of sawdust beneath his boots as he walked across the floor, feeling for a moment almost overwhelmed by the flood of memories, as if he'd stepped back in time fifteen years.

Only two other patrons inhabited the place; these cast him furtive looks that told him he was anything but welcome. He ignored them, hoping he'd get to the bottom of the mystery before long.

A warning voice in his mind rose up, telling him he didn't need any kind of trouble right now. He had had enough. Get out, ride south, don't get involved. He fought the voice down. No, if there was a chance for him here he would take it. Maybe he could finally do some good with the dubious talent God had seen fit to bless him with.

Jake came up to the bar and slid on to a stool. The barkeep, a squat man with tufts of hair that stuck out to either side of his hair-spotted head, glanced at him as if bothered.

'Bourbon,' Jake said, staring the man down. The barkeep seemed to reluctantly reach for the bottle and filled a glass. Jake paid the man and took a gulp, letting the liquor sear his parched throat and quell a bit of uneasiness churning in his gut. 'People 'round here seem a whole lot less friendly than they used to,' Jake added, eyeing the 'keep.

'You been here before?'

'You could say that. It's been a while, but things certainly aren't the way I recall.'

'Things change. The West is dying.'

'You'd almost think so from the way this town looks. What happened? I noticed boarded windows and not much activity on the streets.'

'Nothin',' the barkeep answered with a nervous flutter in his voice. 'Nothin' happened.'

'Could have fooled me.' Jake studied the man's face, seeing deep fear there.

'Look, mister, I don't know who you are or what your business is here, but whatever it is, you'd best drink up and be on your way.'

'You're real encouragin' to the tourism of this town, I bet.' Jake's tone dripped sarcasm. 'So why don't you tell me why I should be going...'

'Like I told you, I don't know nothin'. I find it keeps me healthier that way.'

Jake sighed. The dread feeling he'd

experienced upon riding in was confirmed by the barkeep's words and manner. 'Who's the sheriff here, now? Still Frank Foreman?' He saw the barkeep wince and try to cover it.

'What's it to you?' The 'keep was using belligerence to cover fright, Jake judged.

'Was thinkin' of hiring on as deputy or something. 'Bout the only job I'm qualified for.'

The 'tender let out something close to a laugh. 'Then you danged well better think about changing towns fast.'

'You're just a bundle of optimism, aren't you?' Jake's tone grew serious. 'Now who's the sheriff?'

'Ain't got no sheriff.'

'No?'

'No.' The barkeep reached beneath the counter, pulled up a glass and began to wipe it.

'Why not?' Jake intended to push the man into some answers. The 'keep shrugged.

A soft voice from behind him suddenly

made Jake shiver.

'Jep told me had seen a stranger ride in. Guess he was right.'

Jake felt frozen for a moment, recognizing the voice instantly. As he began to turn, he felt his heart beat in his throat.

The woman, dressed in leather britches, boots, a white blouse covered by a short leather vest, stood with her arms folded just inside the batwing doors. Her blonde hair was tucked under a flat hat, but wisps corkscrewed free about both ears. As she took a few steps forward, Jake had the notion she hadn't changed a bit in fifteen years, his sight gilded by memory.

Nellie Cantrell.

The name rang in his mind like a soft bell. As his sight began to clear, the haze of the past lifting, he spotted a few hard lines that had etched into her face around her eyes and mouth, but she was still every bit as lovely as the day he had left her.

'Well, Jake Donovan, you could at least say hello,' she said, full lips barely moving.

'Danged if you ain't a sight for tired eyes...' he mumbled, feeling tongue-tied.

'It's been a long time...' She stepped up to him and he could smell the flowery scent of her perfume, the same fragrance she'd always loved. A wave of feelings, ancient but warm, washed over him. Leaving Nellie Cantrell had been the hardest thing he'd ever done; seeing her again, though deep in the back of his mind he had prayed he would, had just become the second hardest.

'Fifteen years, three months, twenty-seven days and some odd hours, to be exact.'

'But you weren't counting, right?' She smiled a thin smile and he felt himself want to take her in his arms, hold her the way he used to.

'Not for a moment.'

Nellie pulled out a stool and sat. 'So what brings you back to these here parts? Thought you'd never set foot in Matadero again.'

'Can't say for sure. It sure ain't the hospitality,' Jake cast the barkeep a look.

'Matadero lost its love of strangers,' said Nellie, features going hard. A slight flush lent a rosy look to her cheeks. 'You stayin'?'

'Depends.'

'I'm sure.' A hint of accusation laced her tone. Jake let it pass. He reckoned she might have built up a heap of anger since he left; she had every right to.

'What's going on in this town, Nell?' he asked, hoping to change the subject before she probed too deeply into his motivations for coming back. He realized he had called her Nell, just like that, just slipping back into the old ways like putting on a familiar boot or saddling a favourite horse. It fitted – too well.

'Nothing that don't go on in a lot of small towns – Cardonas are all gone, you know...'

Jake sensed Nellie was as eager to talk about this town as the barkeep. 'I know.'

'That why you're back?' That was Nell, always to the point.

'Partly.'

Jake saw a glint of anger flash in her eyes.

She slid off the stool and started away. Jake suddenly didn't know whether to stop her, though he wanted to; he had no right. She didn't owe him spit.

She stopped a few feet from the doors and half turned. 'Talk to me sometime when you decide what it is you want, Jake Donovan. I've wasted enough of my life pining for old times.' She spun and stalked through the batwings, letting them swing violently behind her. Jake turned back to the bar, blowing out a sigh.

'Told ya it'd be better just to keep goin',' the 'keep said.

'You could be right...'

Jake downed the remainder of his bourbon and headed out. He didn't know what had gotten into this town, but he was determined to find out.

THREE

After departing the Cazador, Jake walked his horse down the street to the livery, wanting to get Zach out of the hot sun, and, since he figured he'd be spending a least a few weeks in Matadero, he'd need a safe place to board the bay. The mystery hanging over this town intrigued him. What was it the people were so skittish about? What had caused a booming Texas town to shrink in on itself the way it obviously had?

Jake thought of Nellie. He couldn't deny the resurgence of familiar warm feelings she had raised up in him. Could he really stay here? Find happiness? Was there any kind of chance for him with Nellie? Heck, he hadn't even bothered to ask her if she was married, he'd been so spellbound by just seeing her again. He couldn't keep her face out of his mind for more than a few moments, it seemed.

But he had to, for the time being anyhow. Something had invaded this town and he was determined to learn what it was.

After boarding Zach, Jake strode along the boardwalk, looking into the small shops and establishments along the street. There was business, he saw, but it seemed so subdued; this surely wasn't the Matadero he remembered. When people spotted him, nervous expressions played on their faces. He knew it wasn't him they were frightened of because few of the townsfolk here now were known to his memory. If anybody recognized him, they kept it to themselves. The only one who could be possibly threatened by his presence, he figured, was old man Cardona, and he was dead. Jake's quarrel hadn't really involved the town, in fact. Mostly it boiled down to the fact that the old man owned Matadero and things had just gotten too uncomfortable after...

Well, this wasn't the time to dwell on that,

was it? If he was going to make a dent in finding out about the strange cloak of fear enwrapping Matadero, he would have to start right away, before the townspeople managed to organize a town-wide silence.

Jake's boots thudded in hollow rhythm as he made his way along the boardwalk, heading towards the first place he could think of finding some answers: the sheriff's office.

Jake halted abruptly, a chill washing down his spine despite the heat of the sun-baked day.

Glancing back over his shoulder, he glimpsed movement as someone disappeared into the alley behind him. Or did he? He couldn't be sure. His hand absently slid over the walnut grip of his Peacemaker. He listened, thought he heard retreating footsteps. As he started towards the alley, mild apprehension fluttered in his belly. Using caution born of years on the open trail, he peered around the corner. The alley was empty! A scorched breeze stirred the dust, but nothing else moved. The blank walls of flanking buildings seemed to mock him. An opening at the opposite end led to a back street, but Jake dismissed investigating it. If anyone had been behind him, he – or she – was gone, now. Jake preferred it that way.

Turning, Jake headed back in the direction he came, unable to shake the feeling someone had been observing him. If someone had, he couldn't guess the reason. It was just one more mystery about this town that would need explaining.

The sheriff's office looked much more ramshackle than he remembered it. Frank Foreman had always kept a respectable house, if he recollected right. Jake twisted the door handle and it felt unusually loose in his hand. The door practically fell open under his push and, gazing down, he could see why. The latch had been torn out and the surrounding wood splintered; the door had been kicked open sometime in the recent past.

Stepping inside, he shut the door behind

him and stood in the ominous gloom of the office.

The place was a wreck. Lead had gouged furrows into the desk and walls. The side windows were missing, shards of glass scattered on the floor beneath the sill. Boards had been haphazardly nailed over the openings. A table was demolished, a tin coffee pot lying on the floor nearby. Beneath the dust, Jake could see brown stains on the boards. He had the sinking feeling they weren't all caused by spilled brew. Near the broken table, a glint of metal caught his eye. Jake went over to it, kneeled, reached out to pick it up. A rusty sheriff's star, he saw, turning the object over in his hand. Foreman's? His gut told him it was.

Palming it, he began to rise, pausing halfway as the feeling of being watched came over him again. He felt hot air brush the back of his neck and suddenly knew someone had eased open the door and was standing in back of him.

Jake had to pull back at the last second,

holding his fire as his sight came upon the portly figure standing in the doorway, a battered felt hat shadowing the features beneath. Jake saw the man was unarmed, but kept the Peacemaker trained on him just the same.

'Who are you?' he asked, keeping his voice steady and gesturing with his shooter.

'You can put that away, Mr Donovan,' the man said with a thick drawl. 'I ain't no danger to you.' As the man stepped into the light, Jake could see he was only about five-five, built like a pickle barrel. The man's features were ruddy, moonlike.

'From what I've seen in this town so far,' said Jake, taking a step forward, 'I'd prefer to get the facts before making that judgement.'

The squat man smiled sheepishly, then reached up and removed his hat. Jake saw the fellow was utterly bald, his pate deeply tanned a reddish bronze from repeated exposure to the hot Texas sun. 'Cain't rightly say I blames you much.' The man gestured towards the desk. 'Mind?'

Jake indicated it was all right. He began to let his guard down a little, instinctively knowing from years on the open trail that this man posed no danger to him.

The man ambled to the desk and slung a stubby leg over its corner, propping himself into a half-sitting, half-standing position on the edge.

'You were observing me, weren't you? In the alley, I mean.'

'Yep, that was me.'

'Why?' Jake holstered his Peacemaker. If the man had posed a serious threat, he would have killed Jake when he had clear shot at him on the street.

'Wanted to see where you was a'goin'.'

Jake cocked an eyebrow. 'And why would you care about that? Seems most of the folk in this town have the exact opposite reaction; they just avoid me and wish I was gone.'

'Not me. I want you to stay, in fact.'

Jake let out a laugh. 'Really? You the

official welcoming committee?'

'No, usually I keep pretty much outa sight, least I does nowadays.'

'You and the rest of this town.' Jake folded his arms.

'They got good reason.'

'That's the problem: I seem to be having a little trouble finding the reason out.' Jake paused, came over to the desk and tossed the rusty star down with a thin clink. 'Sheriff Foreman, what happened to him?' As Jake's gaze fell on the man, the fellow didn't avert his deep-set eyes.

'He's dead.' The man's eyes clouded with a far-off look, but only for a moment. 'Kilt by the Culverin brothers.'

Jake felt something leaden sink in his belly. In his travels, he had heard of the Culverins, knew the things of which the outlaws were capable. If they had invaded this town, that explained a lot.

'You heard of 'em?' asked the barrel-built man, brow wrinkling.

'Oh, yeah. Probably everybody from here

to Cheyenne has. That the reason this town is so locked up?'

'That's the reason.'

Jake sighed. 'Well, it makes sense. I've heard they pick a place and make it their own for a spell, then leave it drained. When did this happen?'

''Bout six months back. You see, they comed in here one day and kilt old Silas at the general store. Kilt the feller for no good reason. They could have took what they wanted. Silas wouldn't raise no hand to stop 'em. But they shot him down in cold blood.'

'That's pretty much in line with what I've heard about them,' Jake agreed.

'Well, then they shot up the town a lick. Sheriff Foreman, me an' a few other deputies headed out after 'em.'

'That's what you call suicide from what I hear.'

'Yep, it was. Ol' Sheriff Frank brung their leader in, but we lost two good men. Then three days later, the rest of 'em got the jump on the sheriff, kilt him. They broke Brent out and went after this town. The sheriff had sent me to take a drunk back to Raco, so I weren't here that night. If'n I had been, well, I wouldn't be talkin' to ya now.'

'Was that the end of it? Was that what frightened these people so much?' Jake couldn't help thinking there was more to it.

'No, no, we ain't that lucky. Every month they come back, headin' up from Raco and a few other towns where they make their usual run. Sometimes one of the varmints comes up a few days early, if'n he ain't got nothin' big in the fire, usually Willie, the young'n. He's got a thing for the ladies.'

Jake felt his stomach tighten and Nellie's face flashed into his mind. 'Thing?'

'Yep, he lines 'em up and takes his pick. They got no call to resist 'cause they know he'd kill 'em.'

'Nellie Cantrell?' Jake blurted before he could stop himself. The thought of one of those outlaws hurting her sent a bolt of anger flashing through his veins like hot lightning.

'Uh-uh. That Nell's a tough cookie, tough

as any man. So far she's been right lucky, though. Only a matter of time 'cause Willie, he's a'runnin' out of choices. The ones he leaves usually ain't no good afterward.' The bald man's gaze dropped.

Jake felt himself sickening at the man's words. 'Why doesn't anybody do anything? I know they're scared, but this whole town against five men, surely–'

The bald man shook his head. 'You don't know 'em! Them hardcases got no souls. The devil made 'em himself.'

Jake nodded, searching his memory. He had a dim recollection of having seen one of the Culverins in action about five years back. Loomis was the outlaw's name, if he remembered right. Jake had been in a saloon about a hundred miles north of Matadero and had seen the brother cheat at a poker game. The cowboy he cheated hadn't even uttered a word, though the deed was blatant. Jake recalled the look of fear in the cowboy's eyes. That was the kind of terror the Culverins bred in a man. Jake hadn't interfered at the time; it wasn't his problem. But now the outlaws had gripped Matadero in their spell and maybe it *would* be his problem if he didn't leave right away. But could he? With Nellie in danger something inside him made him want to risk the very peace he had hoped to find. He had only two options: leave, the way he had fifteen years ago; or stay, and possibly never leave at all.

'What about you?' Jake asked, peering intently at the squat man.

'Name's Abraham Lincoln Hullar. I was a deputy. If the Culverins caught sight of me now, I'd be dead, sure. They think I got my tail outa here six months ago.'

'Why didn't you? I mean, you could have run. It would have been understandable.'

'No, couldn't rightly do that. Ol' Sheriff Foreman, he treated me with more respect than any other ten men. I owed it to him to stay. I kept a'hopin' someday I could do somethin' 'bout the Culverins...'

He bowed his head. 'Over the past few

months I lost most of that hope. All I could do was watch while they tooked what little this town had left.'

'How'd you manage to avoid them?'

'They come pretty much like clockwork. I jest keep low durin' those times. If'n I didn't, I'd be joinin' Sheriff Foreman in Widow's Creek Cemetery.'

Taking a deep breath, Jake walked away from the desk and glanced out the window at the dusty street. In his mind, a struggle had commenced. On one side, old habit told him to leave things be; on the other, the thought of what he wanted to become told him to stay, the part of him that was tired of leaving his life to chance and the wind, the man who wanted desperately to leave behind the years of drifting. Was his answer here in Matadero? Or was death? He was only one man against five; what could he do?

It didn't matter. All the debate in the West couldn't change the notion that had taken hold in his head, birthed at the moment he had sensed the danger looming over this town, and strengthened by what the deputy had just told him. The thought of the Culverins hurting Nellie had sealed it.

In his mind, Jake tried to bring up the image of Brent Culverin. He had seen a picture of the outlaw on a poster once. He didn't think he'd ever be able to forget that hideous face with its repulsive scar. 'Smiley' they called him, with a certain bizarre sense of irony.

'You know who I am, don't you?' he said at last, looking at the deputy.

'Yep. They call you *El Vengador*. I was pretty new here fifteen years back. You probably don't recollect me.'

Jake shook his head; he didn't.

'Anyhow, I heared lots of rumors, heared you were good with that .45 and weren't afeared to use it.' The deputy jabbed a stubby finger at Jake's pistol.

'Rumors are usually just that, rumors. I never use it unless I'm forced to, which might have been a little too often in the past.'

Jake went to the desk, plucked the rusty star from the top. He pinned it to his breast, a vague feeling of pride mixed with unease flowing through him.

'You don't know what you're doin',' said Abe Hullar, the hint of a smile on his lips. 'These boys are as bad as they come. It'd be five against one and each is a crack shot.'

Jake shrugged, wondering secretly if the deputy wasn't right and he was making a huge mistake – one that would end his life. 'How 'bout cutting the odds a bit?' he asked, peering back to the bald man.

'Whatcha mean?'

'Join me. Take back your town like you wanted. This can't go on the way it has, or you'll all wind up dead anyhow.'

'I think you got yourself a deathwish, that's what I think.' The deputy shook his head, but the hint of a smile broadened into a full-fledged grin.

'No, I've got a lifewish. I've done too much driftin' and hiring my gun out for less worthwhile reasons.'

'What makes you think I want a chance at gettin' myself shot to pieces with you?' Amusement filled the deputy's deep-set eyes.

Jake laughed. 'That's what you came here for, isn't it? Hoping I'd help? Besides, you'd have been as far from here as six months could have carried you by now if you didn't want to help.'

Abraham Lincoln Hullar grinned and slapped his hat back on. Pushing himself away from the desk, he started towards the door, pausing with his hand on the handle. Jake eyed him.

'You're right. I was hopin' you'd help.' The deputy's voice turned serious. 'The Culverins show up in three days. Mebbe we should start makin' funeral arrangements just in case. If anything happens to me, I want to be put to rest next to Sheriff Foreman. He was the closest thing to family I had.'

'Three days; that gives us precious little time.' Jake sighed, hoping they could get prepared by then. 'Meet me at the Cazador about five – they still make Texas' best beefsteak and stew there, I take it?'

'You take it right, Mr Donovan. Maybe that pretty little filly will even be there...' The deputy grinned again and Jake chuckled. He had half hoped that.

After the squat deputy departed, Jake sat in the gloomy office, deep in thought. He absently fingered the rusty star, a shred of doubt in his mind. Maybe he couldn't help this town; worse, maybe he couldn't help Nellie or himself. But he owed it to her to at least try. The circle of his life had to close some time.

It looked like now was that time.

FOUR

After retrieving his saddlebag with his belongings – what little there were of them – from the livery attendant, Jake stepped through the doorway into the lobby of the Costanza Hotel. The hostelry was a two-storey structure whose interior was panelled with stained wood; its lobby held furniture that looked as if it had seen better days – stuffing popping chairs, deep gouges in the wood. Two brass chandeliers hung from the high ceiling and Jake could see evidence of cobwebs. He reckoned the Culverins had done nothing for the hostelry's business.

All the way over to the hotel, Jake had found himself recalling his conversation with Deputy Hullar and rethinking the implications of his decision to become sheriff of Matadero. The feeling that he had bitten off far more than he could chew kept surfacing in his mind, no matter how hard he tried to push it out.

Pulling himself from his thoughts and crossing the lobby he reached the desk and rang the bell. A lanky man with dark eyes came from the back room and gave him the once-over, gaze spending an inordinate amount of time glued to the rusty star now pinned to Jake's shirt.

The man with the dark eyes gave a short *ha-umph* and turned around the registration book as if held at gunpoint. Jake studied the proprietor's face: he was white, but the wide set of his dark eyes and the high cheekbones placed him as some sort of breed. Little expression showed on the man's face and Jake couldn't begin to read what was on the hotel man's mind – yet something *was* on it; Jake could tell that much for sure.

'Nobody in this town will lift a hand to help you, you know,' said the man in a deep, even tone. 'They all got a powerful fear and it ain't likely they'll help a stranger – even if he is wearin' a badge.'

'Is that so?' Jake glanced up after signing his name in the book. 'News travels fast, doesn't it?'

The man shrugged. 'News and that star pinned to your shirt. Used to belong to another man who thought about messin' with the Culverins.'

'You're familiar with the Culverins, I take it, Mr...'

'Cross, Jeremy Cross. Did you think anybody in this town wouldn't be?'

'I s'pose not.'

'Originally come from the same piece of country as the Culverins. Don't let them know it, though. It's healthier that way.'

'Lots of people concerned with their individual health in these parts, it seems.' Jake played up the sarcasm in his voice.

'Ain't much choice,' Cross returned with a hint of defensiveness.

'What about you, Mr Cross, would you help?' Jake caught the hotel man's gaze and held it.

'I just run a hotel–' He glanced at the name in the book '–Mr Donovan. That's all. I leave fightin' to those that can.'

'Or will, right? I thought your people had more pride than that. They know better than anyone what it's like to be oppressed.'

'What would you know of them? I am more white–'

'Or yellow,' Jake shot back before he could stop himself. He found the town's lack of willingness to stop the Culverins' threat and help themselves getting on his nerves. He wasn't sure why this bothered him so much, but suspected it had something to do with his own actions fifteen years ago. He didn't particularly care for the face staring back at him from the town's mirror.

The hotel man's face turned crimson, highlighting his Indian features even more. 'You got no call to say that. You haven't lived here–'

'You're right.' Jake held up a hand. 'I got no call. I apologize. But you're wrong on one part, Cross, I have lived here, and when

I did, I ran. That's why this time I gotta do something.' Jake fumbled in his pocket, bringing out some rumpled cash and passing it to the hotel man. The breed counted out just so much then returned the rest to Jake.

'I don't know how long I'll be—'

'You'll be here three days, no more,' Cross said without a glimmer of emotion. Some of the crimson had drained from his face, now.

'How do you know that, might I ask?' Jake didn't like the feeling crawling through his gut.

''Cause that's when the Culverins are due. Past that...' Cross made an Indian cut-off sign. Jake might have laughed if not for the look of utter seriousness on the man's features.

'Glad to see you've got confidence in me, anyway,' Jake quipped, trying to hide the specter of doubt in his voice. Something about the breed's demeanor made him a little uneasy and a whole lot irritated.

'I would not laugh if I were you, Mr

Donovan. Mind you, I have nothing against you personally, but I do not allow myself to become friendly with dead men.' Cross handed Jake the key to his room and Jake headed towards the stairs, an uneasy feeling following him.

'You're just a bundle of upliftin', Mr Cross,' he mumbled, forcing his irritation down. He felt the proprietor's dark eyes bore into his back as he climbed to the second floor.

Opening the door to his room, Jake stepped inside. He tossed the saddle-bag on to the bed and took in the surroundings. Not bad as far as hotel rooms went, he reckoned. He had certainly spent the night in worse accommodations. The patterned wallpaper was peeling a bit and the room had a dingy, slightly dirty look to it, but the small bed looked comfortable, especially after hours in the saddle. He went to the porcelain basin on the bureau and splashed lukewarm water into his face, then towelled off on his untucked shirt, which he stripped off and laid at the foot of the bed. He unbuckled his gunbelt and draped it over a post.

Easing on to the bed, he struggled to relax, realising just how drained the long ride had made him. The adrenalin surge of finding an answer to the mystery of this town and learning the reason behind the rampant fear had worn off. Exhaustion had taken over. He would allow himself a few hours' sleep before meeting Abe at the saloon. That's all he had time for. If the Culverins were due in three days, he had to work fast. He knew it would be a mistake to hit them head-on; he needed some kind of a plan. Another notion played in his mind: he couldn't take just one of them. If one brother remained free, the terror suffocating this town would never end. Brent might be the head of the Culverin body, but Foreman had been, seriously in error if he thought the body couldn't function without it. Jake had dealt with too many hardcases in his life not to know that.

He also resigned himself to the fact that he would have no choice but to use his Peacemaker again. Unless he got real lucky and somehow rounded up the whole gang, it would be impossible to take them alive. Funny, he thought, this time he found himself almost eager to shoot it out with them. The Culverins were vicious killers, and what they had done to this town – besides what they might do – was downright inhuman.

Jake's thoughts began to shift back to Nellie as he felt the disturbed sleep of exhaustion begin to claim him. For a memory, it was as if he had never left Matadero, that he had stayed here all along and everything had worked out as planned between him and Nell fifteen years ago. In a half-dream, he recalled the day before he left, the sun-scorched street and the utter happiness that had clouded his mind, making him oblivious to the threat...

'I'm gonna marry you someday, Jake Donovan,' Nellie said, smiling up at him, as they walked hand in hand down the boardwalk. She wore a bright blue dress embroidered with yellow and white flowers; she had made it herself. Her long blonde hair tumbled loose at her shoulders and Jake had to admit she was just the prettiest sight he'd ever laid eyes on.

'You're probably right, Nell,' he said, surprised at finding himself not all that averse to the idea. 'But with Miguel Cardona around ... I don't think he's gonna let you go so easy.'

'Miguel's a fool if he thinks I could ever marry the likes of him. His father thinks he owns this town–'

'He does! At least half the property and a few of the officials, anyhow. The old man donates a hefty amount of cash to the padre, too, don't forget.'

'Father Jasper's mostly honest. I think he relies on the Cardona money, but he'd still marry us.'

She gazed at Jake and he felt a shiver go through him at the look in her eyes.

'Years ago, the Cardona family made an arrangement with my pa,' she continued. 'Gave him a lot of money when his ranch was failing. Guess my pa had nothing to promise 'cept me. But pa's gone now and so is the ranch. I got no reason to hold to a promise I had no choice in – and the old man's got no claim on me, neither.'

Jake shook his head. 'That's not what Miguel thinks. In his opinion, he owns you lock, stock and barrel. I heard him making a lot of noise about it at the Cazador the other night. Could be trouble.'

'It don't matter, Jake. The only thing that matters is what we feel for each other. We can leave this town, go up to Dodge or someplace and start over. Please, Jake. You love me too, I know it!'

Jake felt his heart sink. He found himself desperately wanting to run away with her, start over, but something always held him back. What? He loved her, more than anything, but the restless part of his soul was struggling for dominance. And to face the wrath of the Cardonas, well, that made him more than a little reluctant, too, though he suspected that was mostly an excuse.

'I don't know, Nell. I just don't know. It's what I want, but...'

'But what? Do you love me, Jake Donovan? Tell the truth, 'cause I'd know it if you lied and I want to know if I'm wastin' my time.'

He turned to her, gazing deep into her china-blue eyes. When he stared into their depths it was as if nothing else mattered, nothing else at all, not the Cardonas, not his restless spirit. But when he looked away ... well, then the doubts would creep in, and the wanderlust. 'Yes, I do love you, Nell,' he answered finally, the truth. 'More than anything.'

'Then you'd better decide, Jake, and soon. 'Cause pretty soon Miguel is gonna come callin' and his father ain't one to cotton to the word *no*.'

'I know.' Jake bowed his head, his mind in turmoil, torn between what he wanted and what wanted him. Nellie stood on her tiptoes and kissed his cheek, then walked off, heading in the direction of the small clapboard place she called her home at the edge of town. He watched her go, kicking himself for not running after her and telling her right away that they could get married as soon as the sun came up on a new day. What was holding him back?

Dang it! he thought, as he started down the boardwalk, intending to go into the Cazador. He passed an alley, paying no attention to it, confined to the struggle in his mind.

Something slammed into the back of his head. Something hard! A stream of stars streaked across his vision and his mind reeled. Strong arms clamped about his chest, pinning his arms, flung him face first to the dirt of the alley floor. Dust mixed with the coppery-salt flavour of his blood tasted bitter on his tongue; he had bitten his lips when he'd crashed into the ground. A sharp pain lanced his ribs and he realized the attacker had stamped him with a boot for good measure.

'Get up, *amigo!*' a young, Spanish-laced voice commanded.

Jake coughed a mouthful of dirt and blood and made a shaky effort at gaining his feet. His head took a moment to stop spinning, but he managed to find his balance and stand. He turned to face his assailant.

Instantly he recognized the swarthy features of Miguel Cardona. He was dressed in an expensive, Spanish-styled suit, but a gunbelt hung at his hips. He had a Smith & Wesson levelled at Jake's chest, an itchy finger unstill on the trigger. Jake knew he was very close to death.

'Usually I don't work this out in the open, Donovan, but extreme cases call for extreme measures.' Miguel's face twisted with a look of contempt.

'Usually you have your daddy do it for you,' Jake shot back impulsively, instantly regretting it.

'*Mula!*' The young man jumped forward and swung the Smith & Wesson at Jake's jaw.

Jake saw it coming, but was still too dazed to avoid the blow completely. The gun cracked against his chin in a glancing blow. Jake felt a welt of pain and more blood poured into his mouth. He reeled, staggering backward and crashing heavily against the wooden wall of the building. Flinging his arms out reflexively, he used the wall for support. If it had not been there, he would have gone down again.

Miguel laughed. 'Well, Senor Donovan, what does it take to make you leave our Miss Cantrell alone? *Que?* Maybe some money, eh? Maybe a lot of money. That's what your kind usually goes for, no? *Cuanto cuesta?* How much? Maybe a little extra for you to leave town completely?'

'You're wrong, Cardona,' Jake said through clenched teeth, wiping blood away from his mouth with the back of his hand. 'I'm not leaving Nellie. And you're not having her!'

'Oh, come, come, now, Senor Donovan. I know your type better than you know yourself. You all have a price. No woman's worth it to a man like you. Name it, make it easy on both of us.'

Anger flashed in Jake's eyes. 'You don't know spit, Cardona. You think because your father's got so much pull you can waltz in here and take whatever you want. You've always had everything handed to you, but not Nellie. Your father's bought you out of plenty of trouble, but if you so much as touch her there's no amount of money that'll keep me from making you pay. She'll be marrying me, so you better just get used to it.'

Miguel spat and gave a derisive laugh. 'I thought you were smarter than that, Donovan, at least where your own hide was concerned. But perhaps I was mistaken, yes? Listen well, *amigo*, because I'm only going to tell you this one time: Stay away from Nellie Cantrell or I'll kill you. *Comprende?*' Miguel jabbed the Smith & Wesson under Jake's chin, forcing his head up, and glared at him. Sweat dribbled down Jake's face and blood leaked from his lips.

Uttering a cruel laugh, Miguel swung the gun up in a vicious arc and cocked Jake in the temple. The world flashed to black, then came back again, but Jake was already crumbling to the ground. His head whirled, only for a moment this time. Through blurred vision he saw the young Cardona turn his back and begin to walk from the alley, holstering his Smith & Wesson and laughing.

Anger surged through Jake's veins. He knew why Nellie would have nothing to do with the spoiled arrogant son of Diego Cardona. They were outlaws, fancy ones, but still outlaws. Oh the father was a shade better, only responsible for pulling a few shady deals, mostly just getting what he wanted by throwing around his money and by intimidation; but the son, the son was a hardcase with a silver spoon in his mouth. He would kill Jake if Jake let him. Jake was danged if he'd let Nellie face a life with the likes of him, of that he was certain.

Weakness flooding him, legs quivering,

body objecting at every turn, Jake forced himself to his feet. Drawing deep breaths, he took a few staggering steps forward, gaining strength more quickly than he thought he would.

The young Cardona had reached the mouth of the alley.

'Cardona!' Jake shouted, blood running from his lips. The young man turned, a vicious look welded to his face, one he usually kept hidden, but one that showed his true nature.

Jake's hand quivered a foot away from his gun. The young man grinned a knowing grin.

'If that's the way you want it, Senor Donovan ... I'd prefer it. I would have killed you sooner or later anyway, so it might as well be now. *Draw!*'

Jake' s vision blurred! A beat. Through the haze he caught the jerk of the young man's hand towards his Smith & Wesson. Jake had no choice; he couldn't let his lack of clearheadedness hinder him now. He was already committed.

Jake's hand flashed for his gun, a blur.

The young Cardona's fingers met the Smith & Wesson's butt, clamped to it and began to pull it free. He was fast, Jake thought. Very fast.

But not fast enough.

Jake levered his .45 before the young man's gun cleared its holster. His vision flashed clear and he saw the look of surprise that welded on to Miguel's face as he jerked back, gun tumbling to the dirt. The young man's surprise turned to shock when he looked down at the scarlet blotch spreading across his chest.

The echo of Jake's gunshot reverberated from the wooden walls and thundered back at him. In slow motion, he saw Miguel crumble to the street, saw people rush towards the fallen man.

Jake stumbled forward, still half-dazed, but not numbed enough not to realize he had just made his life's biggest mistake. He had gunned down Miguel Cardona. From this point onward the father would never let Jake have a moment's peace. Jake might just as well have shot himself.

Reaching Cardona's side, he prayed hopelessly there was a chance the wound hadn't been fatal. But he knew it had to be; when Jake Donovan shot at something, it was generally a perfect hit.

In the remaining hours of that day, everything came to pass the way Jake thought it would. Diego Cardona, furious at the loss of his only son, had sworn he'd make Jake's life a living hell if he didn't leave town immediately. Although the sheriff had accepted Jake's explanation of self-defence – he had experienced enough dealings with the young Cardona to be almost glad to be rid of him – Foreman also knew bucking the older Cardona was serious business. He suggested things might be easier if indeed Jake found other pastures.

Jake hadn't slept all that night, knowing what would have to happen the next day. The rising sun found him and Nellie at the edge of town, standing side by side. He could see the look of hurt in her china-blue eyes, the look of knowing that this was the end for them.

'Please, Jake, let me go with you,' she pleaded. 'There's nothing for me here.'

Jake's throat tightened and a searing pain went through his heart. 'There's no life for you there.' He pointed toward the open trail. 'Whatever it was holding me back from marrying you before is stronger now. I have to face it alone.'

'Jake ... don't...' A tear slipped down her face and her hands went to her trembling lips. Close to tears himself, he felt as if something deep inside were tearing his guts apart, but he forced himself to mount his horse and turn away. He began to ride, not daring to look back, because if he did, in an instant of weakness he might take her with him. He had to be strong, he told himself. He couldn't destroy two lives, and the open trails of a drifter were no place for a woman like Nellie Cantrell. He hoped she would forget and find happiness without him. He knew he'd never forget her.

'I'm gonna marry you someday, Jake Donovan!' he heard her yell through the tears.

He choked back his sorrow. 'I pray to God you're right,' he mumbled, lips tight. 'I pray to God you're right.'

The memory of that time fifteen years ago came flooding back into Jake's half-sleep like the raging torrent of a river, overwhelming him. He jerked awake, sitting bolt upright. Swinging his legs off the bed and putting his face into his hands, he sat alone with his thoughts and sorrows.

'You were the world's biggest fool, Jake Donovan,' he mumbled. 'Letting that girl get away. The world's biggest fool. But what now?'

Was there a chance for them after all this time and pain? Would the Culverins even let him take it if it were there?

Right now, he just didn't know.

FIVE

'You treated him a mite rough from what I hear,' said Nellie Cantrell, giving the barkeep, whose name was Ben, a disparaging look. 'Jake Donovan's the one man who might be able to do somethin' for this town.'

The barkeep shrugged. 'Look, no need of nobody else gettin' killed by the Culverins. The less he knows the better for him – and us!' He finished wiping out a glass and set it beneath the counter.

'Jake already knows.'

The barkeep let out a sigh. 'What? How?'

'Things get around, even in a shut-up town like this.' Nellie eyed the keep mischievously. 'Jake pinned Foreman's star to his chest, I heard.'

A worried look slapped the barkeep's face. 'Tarnation! That's just what we need. The

Culverins'll take it out on us all if he gives them any trouble. You mark my word, young lady!'

Nellie laughed. 'Funny thing is, you probably got him to stay yourself.' She gave Ben a sarcastic smirk. The barkeep could use a little toying with, she figured. Maybe it would help Jake in the long run if she gave the 'keep a healthy dose of guilt.

'How's that?' Nellie saw his worried look increase.

'Well, just by clammin' up you made him all the more curious. If I know Jake, that probably hasn't changed a bit in fifteen years.' Nellie suddenly wondered if anything else had. Perhaps she'd find out. 'Maybe the Culverins will give you some special consideration for that.' She controlled the urge to grin.

The barkeep gave a shudder. 'Don't you go playin' with me, Nellie Cantrell. You still ain't too old to take over my knee.'

Nellie let out an easy laugh. She had known the barkeep since she was a little girl, back when he had worked for her father on the ranch. She'd even called him Uncle Ben when she was small. But now, she found his run-scared attitude irked her powerfully. She was dog-tired of the fear gripping this town and she was fed up with the Culverins and their raids. She'd seen the scars they left on the people's souls. If Jake Donovan had a chance of putting a stop to that, she could at least do her best to drum up some support, despite her feelings for him. Besides, right now she didn't know what to think about his coming back. She felt too much hurt – and hope – to dwell on possibilities and long-forgotten dreams.

'I'd like to see you try!' She smiled a playful smile, then added, 'You keep fearin' the Culverins like that and you'll lose the rest of your hair!'

The barkeep shook his tufted head, about to respond when the clamor of beating hooves grabbed his attention. Noises drifted in from the street: a shot, a scream and a grating laugh that sounded almost demonic.

A whoop followed, sending a shiver down Nellie's spine.

'Oh-oh,' she muttered, lips drawing into a tight line.

The worried look on the barkeep's face changed to one of subtle terror. 'One of 'em's early again,' he mumbled, staring towards the batwings.

'Willie, I bet.' Nellie felt her heart leap. 'He usually comes around the dinner hour, lookin' for food and...' She let her words trail off. So far she had been luckier than most of the younger girls of Matadero, but if she didn't leave the Cazador in a hurry, her luck might just run out. She crossed the sawdust-covered floor in four long steps. She couldn't deny the bolt of fear that struck her whenever the Culverins came riding in. She was no more immune to their spell than the other townsfolk.

A thought struck her: one brother showing up early might seriously hinder Jake's plan, if he had one. She took the notion to warn him before that could happen.

Nellie stopped short at the entrance. The batwing doors slowly pushed wide, Willie Culverin framed in the dusty sunlight filtering in from the street, a vicious look lashing like bullwhips in his eyes. He looked like a nightmare to her, something unreal and evil. She felt her mouth go dry and her heart start to pound.

'Where y'all goin' in such a all-fired hurry, little lady?' asked the nightmare. She took a small step backward. 'Be mighty rude if'n ya didn't sit down with old Willie for a drink, doncha think?' He grinned a demon grin.

'I got nothin' to say to you, Willie Culverin.' Nellie forced her voice to remain steady and tried to swallow her heart, which was lodged in her throat. 'Now get out of my way before I–'

'Before you what?' he interjected, stepping forward. His hand shot out and went to the back of her neck, grabbing her and jerking her close. Nellie winced in pain as the outlaw's fingers dug into her flesh, but then gritted her teeth, not wanting to give the hardcase the satisfaction of hearing her cry out.

'Let me go, you no-good!' she yelled, trying to boot the hardcase in the shin. He laughed, mocking her, and pulled his leg out of the way before she could do any damage. His fingers tightened and she gave up her kicking.

'Had my eye on you fer quite a spell, truth is.' Willie pulled her along with him as he made his way into the room. 'Just savin' the best for last – how 'bout it, barkeep, you think this little filly and me make a downright pretty couple?' The stench of old whiskey on the outlaw's breath assailed her nostrils. It repulsed her, as did everything about the youngest Culverin. He was as bad – maybe worse – than the leader in some ways, she knew, especially where the ladies were concerned.

The barkeep's face had turned red. Nellie knew he was struggling to hold back his anger, but without much success. 'Don't, Ben, not now! It ain't worth it–'

Willie Culverin sneered and gave a hearty jerk on her neck. She bit her lip, holding back a cry.

'Don't Ben,' the youngest Culverin mocked. 'It ain't worth it. Why, I get the impression you don't think we make a pretty couple, you old hog. In fact, I get the notion you don't like me very much at all. I'd hate it if you didn't like me. Hurts me right here.' With a fist he thumped his chest over his heart and grinned wider. 'Come on, you washed-up old coot! Play hero and save the little lady. Ain't got no guts?' The outlaw yanked Nellie's neck again, this time so hard she couldn't hold back a bleat of pain. She aimed another kick at the hardcase's shin, but he swung her around and her boot went wide.

'Why you no-good bushwhacker!' Ben spat through gritted teeth. He dived for the Winchester hidden beneath the bar.

'No!' Nellie screamed as she saw him move. She had wanted him to stand up to the gang, but not with the odds so against him.

A fevered look flashed from Willie Culverin's eyes.

The barkeep swung the Winchester up, levered it as Nellie began to struggle furiously, trying to bite, kick, gouge, but the outlaw pinned her to him, oblivious to the damage she was inflicting.

Willie's free hand streaked for his Colt. Snapping it up, he blasted off a shot before the barkeep, who had to be careful not to hit Nellie, could get a decent aim.

The sound of Culverin's shot crashed like a cannon in Nellie's ear. The instant sorrow of seeing the barkeep fly back into the shelves of bottles, a huge red spot ripening on his shirt, pierced her like rattlesnake fangs. She screeched and intensified her struggles, trying to wrench the Colt from the outlaw's grip.

Behind the bar, the 'keep crumpled to the floor, a sea of shattered bottles, spilled liquor and blood washing over the floor around his dead form.

The Culverin brother rasped out a laugh

and swung Nellie around, his hand lashing out and cuffing her full across the face. 'C'mon, girlie-girl, you gotta start bein' nicer to old Willie. I get powerful mad when my ladies ain't sweetlike.'

'Let her go...' a shaky voice said from behind the young outlaw. Willie froze and Nellie felt a spark of relief. Slowly turning, Willie Culverin faced the short barrel form of Deputy Abraham Lincoln Hullar, who was standing just inside the batwing doors, hands poised to go for the guns now strapped to his ample waist. 'I said let her go.' The deputy's voice was steadier this time.

'Get out, Abe!' Nellie shouted. 'Get Jake–' The outlaw yanked Nellie back, snapping off her words.

'Well, well, lookie here. Thought you'd hightailed it to one of them prissy eastern towns where they ain't got no backbones, you yella-belly. You cain't have no guts so it must be stupidity bringin' you into my sight.'

Nellie saw Abe's face redden, but the

portly deputy held his ground. 'Abe, go, please, get Jake–'

'Shut up!' yelled the outlaw, anger shoving away the cocky attitude he'd sported a moment before. 'Just shut up or I'll kill ya right now!'

Abe took a step forward. The outlaw's Colt jerked level. 'Stop right where you are, fat boy! Don't know where you came by your burst of guts, but it'll get you dead mighty quick if you keep a comin'. I'm runnin' out of patience. Now, who's this Jake feller she's blabbin' about?'

'Jake Donovan, the new sheriff,' answered Abe, face bleached.

'Don't mean nothin' to me,' said Willie, spitting. 'But if you want to get him I'd be right glad to kill him for ya, just like I did that used-up saddle-bag, Foreman.'

'Why you – let her go, you coward!' Abe took her another step forward.

'Surely...' The youngest Culverin grinned and flung Nellie aside. She spun, slammed into a table, catching the edge and managing to keep her feet. In horror, she saw the outlaw's gun level and knew Abe had no chance…

Jake Donovan pushed himself off the bed. He had been unable to sleep, despite his exhaustion, his mind too cluttered with thoughts of the past and misgivings about the future. He had only three days in which to devise some sort of plan against the Culverins or his play as sheriff would be useless. Trouble was, he couldn't think of anything. He'd always faced his enemies head on. Long term set-up wasn't his cup of tea.

Five Culverins; two of them, himself and Abe. Not great odds. He doubted Abe would be much help in an open fight. Probably more of a hindrance, in fact. He shook his head, feeling his confidence dissolve.

Going to the basin, Jake splashed water on his face, then towelled off with linen he'd found in the water closet. After, he went to the window and peered out at the sun, judging from its position it was close enough to five to be on his way to the Cazador to meet Abe. Perhaps the deputy had come up with something. At the least, Abe could furnish Jake with more details about the way the Culverins operated when they rode through Matadero.

Turning away from the window and starting across the room, Jake halted as sounds reached his ears; a shot, a scream, beating hooves that abruptly ended, then a whoop. A chill swept through him. He knew from years of trail-honed instinct what was up. Abe had told him one of the Culverins sometimes rode in early; Jake reckoned that was it. Well, that was more to his liking. One on one was nice and evenlike, and Jake had the advantage – he knew the outlaw was here; the reverse wasn't true.

Jake checked the cylinder of his Peace-maker, finding it loaded. Clicking the chambers shut, he reholstered the weapon. He went to his saddle-bag and pulled out his Bowie knife, strapping it to his side.

Exiting the room, he trotted down the hall and descended the steps. As he crossed the lobby, he noticed Jeremy Cross staring after him, face a blank.

'You'd best stay in your room, Donovan. Lots healthier for us all that way.'

'Yeah?' said Jake, not missing a stride. 'I'll keep that in mind.' He pushed through the doors into the sweltering late-afternoon sunlight. He scanned the street, but all seemed quiet now. 'What the...'

Then he noticed an unfamiliar horse tethered to the rail outside the Cazador, a roan, packing two rifles. Only one horse. Good, that's the way he liked it.

Stepping off the boardwalk, he crossed the street and sidled along the opposite buildings towards the saloon. It was too quiet, he reckoned. That made him edgy. Something was wrong, and Jake felt a tingling of apprehension in his belly.

He reached the Cazador, slowly manoeuvring into a position against the building front where he could see in the right-hand window.

127

The scene within chilled him. He saw Nellie in the grip of the outlaw – he couldn't be sure which brother though he knew it wasn't Brent or Loomis, the one he'd seen at the poker game. Standing just inside the doorway, a little off to the left, he saw Abe, the deputy's hands ready to go for his guns. 'Crazy fool...' Jake muttered, admiring the barrel-built man's courage, but knowing the outlaw would gun him down before he even cleared the holster.

Jake began trying to figure ways to get Nellie far enough out of the line of fire so he could trigger a clear shot at the hardcase. The problem suddenly solved itself as he heard Abe's voice filter through the doorway, telling the outlaw to let the girl go. He saw the Culverin fling Nellie away–

Jake bolted into motion. He had a split second before the outlaw gunned down Abe!

Bursting through the batwings, Jake's hand swept to the Peacemaker.

Abe's hand was on his gunhandle, but

moving far too slow. The Culverin had already drawn a bead on the deputy's wide chest.

At Jake's entrance, the hardcase's attention snapped towards him. Surprise slipped across the outlaw's stubbly face. He tried desperately to jerk his Colt around to fire at Jake, but didn't take enough time to aim. A slug plowed into the wall inches from Jake's head, splintering wood. Jake heard the shriek of the bullet flying past his ear.

Jake's finger eased the trigger in. The Peacemaker boomed. Surprise flashed to shock on the outlaw's features as a slug took him square in the chest and hurled him backward over a table.

Silence.

Abe peered at Nellie, whose features were still drawn taut with fear, then at Jake, who stared at the unmoving form of the outlaw. Jake made sure there wasn't even a twitch from the gunman because the hardcase had somehow managed to retain his grip on the Colt and Jake couldn't afford any errors in judgement at this point. A wrong step could mean instant death for him, Nellie or Abe.

He edged inward, manoeuvring around the tables until he reached the sprawled form of Willie Culverin. Nudging the hardcase with a boot toe, Jake searched for any signs of life, keeping his Peacemaker trained on him the whole time. The outlaw's form was limp, so Jake holstered his gun and knelt, turning the body on to its back. The hardcase's arms flopped sideways and Jake could see that he was dead. Jake Donovan usually didn't miss and this time proved no exception.

Jake studied the boy – he couldn't have been much more than twenty-two, despite the hardness that made his face look years older than it should have. He felt regret well at having to kill one so young, but the outlaw had given him no choice. He knew when he decided to pin the star on his chest it would come down to this, but that didn't make it any easier.

Abe and Nellie came up behind Jake but

he didn't move for a moment.

'You OK, Jake?' asked Nellie, hand going to his shoulder.

'Yeah, fine.' He stood, drawing in a deep breath.

'He killed poor Ben, if that makes a difference,' said Nellie, tears glossing her eyes. 'He was gonna kill me 'til Abe came along.'

Jake gave the deputy a thankful nod and the lawman tipped his hat in acknowledgement.

'What about the others?' asked Abe.

'What about 'em?' said Jake, going to the bar and looking at the dead form of the barkeep, a sick feeling flooding his belly. He took an unbroken bottle of bourbon from the floor, sat on a stool and took a long drink. The liquor burned his throat but did little to quell the uneasy feeling he always got around death.

Abe ambled up to the bar, shot a glance at the barkeep, then quickly averted his gaze, obviously bothered by the sight. Nellie stood rigid, arms folded, as if not trusting her emotions if she ventured over near Ben.

'I mean, they're gonna be downright angered now that you kilt their youngest.'

So, it was Willie Culverin dead on the floor, Jake thought. He had guessed that much by the outlaw's apparent age. 'Good. The madder they get, the more likely they are to be reckless. At least the odds are going down. It'll only be four against two, now.'

'Four against three,' said Nellie, drawing her lips into a tight line.

'What?' asked Jake and Abe in unison, as they turned towards her.

'Four against three. They killed Ben and threatened me. I'm tired of living in fear.'

'No, I won't hear of it.' Jake gestured forcefully with his hand.

'You can't stop me, Jake Donovan. You know I can hold my own with a gun better'n most men, and no one else in this hootenanny town is going to raise a finger against the Culverins. They're all too scared.' A determined look welded on to her face and Jake knew nothing he could say would deter her from joining him and Abe. In one way, he was glad for it, because she *was* better with a six-shooter than most men and almost certainly better than the squat deputy, who certainly made up for in courage what he lacked in skill; in another aspect, it scared the hell out of him. He hadn't come back to Matadero after all these years just to lose her again.

'I don't suppose I can change your mind?' he grumbled, taking another slug of bourbon.

'You know me better'n that, Jake Donovan.'

'Yeah, I'm afraid I do.'

Nellie turned on a boot toe and stalked across the barroom, then out through the doors. Jake knew she was on her way to arm herself.

'Feisty little gal, that one,' ventured Abe, shaking his head.

'Maybe too feisty for her own good,' mumbled Jake. Then, looking up at the deputy, he added, 'Get a wagon over here for the 'keep; at least we can give him a decent burial before the rest of the gang shows up.'

'What about that piece of dirt?' asked Abe, nudging his head towards the dead outlaw. 'Same thing?'

'No, not yet. We might find some use for him.' Jake found a vague notion turning over in his mind, one that would call for using the dead outlaw as a weapon against other members of the band. He just hadn't figured out quite how yet.

Abe gave him a quizzical look mixed with a little revulsion.

'Find a nice cool cellar to store him in for the time being,' Jake added.

With that, Jake thunked the bourbon on the bar, had second thoughts and grabbed the bottle and headed out towards the hotel. For a while the liquor was the only company he planned on needing.

SIX

The next day found Jake Donovan, Abraham Lincoln Hullar and Nellie Cantrell starting preparations for the arrival of the Culverin brothers in two days. Most arrangements had been minor, mostly consisting of boarding up shop and establishment windows to prevent as much damage as possible in an all-out gunfight. To Jake, it seemed like dang little, but it was a start. The group had encountered stares and frightened looks from the townspeople, but no resistance. Jake had reached the conclusion that if they were going to take this town back from the outlaws they would have to do it on their own. It irked him that Jeremy Cross had been annoyingly accurate in his prediction. Jake supposed he couldn't blame the folk, but it *was* their town after all;

he thought they'd be at least mildly interested in helping with the securing of their property. He chalked it up to their being more afraid of the Culverins' wrath than of the potential damage.

Jake and Abe also scouted every inch of the town. If they were forced to retreat, he wanted to be sure of the safest places.

By noon, they'd issued an ultimatum to the townsfolk: be prepared to help out or hide out. Jake didn't want anyone innocent getting in the way and being used as a possible shield, the way Willie had used Nellie.

Nightfall found Jake retiring to his hotel room. Jeremy Cross cast him a beady, knowing look as Jake climbed the stairs to his room. He was dead tired, but found himself unable to get even a wink of sleep. His mind raced with the impending arrival of the gang, as well as the myriad contrary emotions that returning to Matadero and finding Nellie again had brought him.

What if he did clear out the Culverins?

Jake asked himself. What then? Did he go on being sheriff of this cowpoke town? Could he stay this time? Or would that restless pull of the open trail send him drifting again? And what about Nell? She had stayed strangely silent all day, going about her work and saying hardly an unrelated word to him. He found that just being close to her made him uneasy; his feelings for her from fifteen years ago were still there. Could he face the thought of leaving her again? Would she even give him a second chance after the way he had left her? Hurt her?

Jake shook his head and swung his feet off the edge of the bed, getting himself into a sitting position. He was too edgy to rest any longer. Glancing at the half-empty bottle of bourbon on the bureau, he considered finishing it, then decided against it. It wouldn't help. It wouldn't wash away the decision he knew he'd have to make when this was over.

He got up, pacing the floor for endless minutes, then went to the window and looked out onto the darkened street. Patches of blue-black shadows flittered here and there, as the tepid breeze stirred tarps, awnings or hanging clothes. He stared in the direction of Raco, feeling a wave of apprehension sweep up from the forbidding trail and blow through him. He knew why these people held such fear of the Culverins; it was almost infectious. He felt it all too deeply himself.

Jake turned away from the window, the thought of heading out for a walk to clear his mind rattling around in his head when he heard the soft tapping of knuckles on his hotel door. He halted, hand reaching for his Peacemaker and pulling it loose. He wasn't in the mood to take chances, not this close to the Culverins' arrival.

'Who is it?' he asked in a soft tone, pressing himself against the wall beside the door and waiting for a response.

'Jake ... it's me...' a soft feminine voice returned and suddenly he felt a little foolish. He holstered his Peacemaker and pulled the door open.

'Nell...' he whispered.

She was wearing the blue dress embroidered with white and yellow flowers he remembered from years ago – no, he corrected, that wasn't quite right: it was merely one much like it. Memory had clouded his vision again. In the weak amber light from the kerosene wall lamp, she looked an angel of loveliness, long blonde hair loose and falling over her shoulders, a twinkle of flame reflected in her china-blue eyes. She looked down coyly, then back up to him.

'There's a dance at Jasper's Hall. Couple of folks decided to tie the knot and head on up to Okie before the Culverins come ridin' in. Can't say I blame them ... can't say I don't envy them just a bit... Well, I was wondering if'n you weren't busy and all ... well, maybe you'd like to take me. We don't have much time 'til...'

'That's my Nell, always right to the point.' As soon as the words tumbled from his mouth, Jake almost regretted saying 'my Nell'. It had just come out so natural. But she wasn't his anymore, perhaps had never been or never would be. He felt relieved when she didn't say anything about the slip.

'Not that I'm saying we won't come through this...'

'The odds are against us,' said Jake. 'I'm not afraid to face up to that.'

'I know, but in case ... I mean, I just don't want it to be like it was today, us – mostly me – not talking to each other like nothin' ever happened between us. It might be a short spell together, but I want what there is of it.'

'Nell, I...' he started, not knowing what to say or feel, but suspecting something deep in his heart had already settled it for him.

'No, you don't have to say anything,' she said, placing a finger to his lips. 'I didn't come here to ask for explainations or promises. Just for a dance.'

'I'd be honored, Nellie Cantrell,' said Jake, meaning it. He slipped on his Stetson then took her arm, escorting her down the hall and steps. This drew a dour look from Jeremy Cross and Jake found himself growing more and more annoyed at the proprietor.

'Don't you have anything better to do?' he asked, as they crossed the lobby.

The hotel man shrugged, a ghost of a smirk spreading over his lips. 'Ain't had a whole lot of business since the Culverins came callin'. Now that you're gonna call them out, I s'pect there'll be even less.'

Jake shook his head and let Nellie pull him to the door.

Jasper's Hall was a ramshackle affair on the edge of town. It was used mostly for town gatherings, weddings, sometimes funerals – business must have picked up on that front, Jake thought wryly, since the Culverins had blown in – and dances. A small band consisting of two fiddlers, a guitar and a squeeze box played spritely Mexican music. Jake had always been fond of that and he and Nellie danced every dance. Jake found it did wonders taking his mind off the Culverins, but, as the band shifted into a slow, sorrowful tune, he also found his head crowded with thoughts of the beautiful woman in his arms. If felt so good to hold her again, so much like old times, before Miguel Cardona. He cursed himself for leaving her in the first place, double cursed himself for thinking he might have to do it again if he didn't wind up in a pine box in two days.

'Jake,' said Nellie, looking up at him. Lamplight shined from her eyes and her face looked radiant in the topaz glow. 'Will you be stayin' after ... well, I know I said I wouldn't ask no questions, but I waited for you, Jake, always hoping there was some slim chance you might come back. I reckon I coulda married, but no one seemed to live up to you in my mind. It's been a lot of years...'

'I know. I guess in my own way I waited for you, too. I know that doesn't make sense, but weren't many a day gone by when you didn't come on my mind.'

Nellie smiled, full lips soft and appealing in the warm light. 'I wondered all along what I'd say if you did come back. In my mind I went over it a hundred times. I wanted to yell at you for leavin' like that, and I wanted to tell you my feelings and anger, but when it came down to it and I saw you standin' in the Cazador yesterday, I just felt all balled up inside.'

'Me, too,' whispered Jake, swallowing hard at the emotion holed up in his throat.

'Please, Jake, tell me you're stayin'.'

He swallowed again, wishing he could give her the answer she wanted to hear – the one maybe he wanted just as bad. 'I can't promise ... I can't, Nell. I've been on the road too long; it gets into your blood like the consumption and stays with you...'

'Or kills you...'

She looked into his eyes.

'Or kills you.' Jake felt a chill shatter the warmth of the moment and pulled her closer, as if to protect himself from his own restless spirit. For the remainder of the song they danced in silence.

The band ended its set and Jake saw the bridal couple move to the back of the spacious room preparing to leave. Looks of restrained happiness played on their faces. Their fear of the Culverins staining the moment, Jake reckoned. He saw Nellie looking at them, too, and felt a vague uneasiness come over him at the smile that spread on to her lips.

'It's getting late,' he said hastily, pulling her attention away from the couple. 'We'd best be on our way.'

Leaving the hall, they strolled down the darkened street in silence and Jake could hear the lonesome chirps and calls of night creatures echoing in from the hills. It filled him with a forlorn feeling, an echo of everything that was a part of him, the drifting, the call of the trail. Nellie slid in closer to him, her form comforting, subduing the restlessness burning in his soul.

'I had a nice time, Jake. After all these months of living in fear it felt so good to be happy again. Being with you brought back some good feelings.'

'I feel the same way, Nell.'

'I wish it didn't have to end...' She lowered her head, a serious look on her face.

'Don't you worry. We're gonna come out of this just fine. The Culverins are mostly reputation. They might just turn tail and run soon as somebody faces up to them.'

'Do you really believe that?' Nellie asked, doubt in her voice.

Jake didn't answer.

'What about us, Jake; will *we* come through this?' She faced straight ahead and Jake felt ice pool in the pit of his heart. Again he didn't answer.

They reached the porch of her small house and Jake walked her up to the door.

She turned towards him and he kissed her on the cheek. Smiling, she opened her door as he went down the steps.

'I'm gonna marry you someday, Jake

Donovan,' he heard her suddenly call from behind him. 'I said it fifteen years ago and I'm saying it now.'

Jake turned back to her, but he saw the door gently closing. Gazing at the portal, he shook his head and smiled, finding himself nowhere near as averse to the notion as he had been earlier in the evening.

'If I don't get myself killed in two days...' he whispered, only half-joking.

Jake headed back into town, intending to retire to his hotel room for the night. He felt much more at ease, now. As his boots clogged on the boardwalk, his mind was filled with the events of the past few hours, Nell and the dance, old feelings.

He had travelled about half the distance to the Costanza when a wave of apprehension shattered the peaceful mood he'd been lulled into – the same sense of being followed, watched, as he had experienced his first day in Matadero. Then, it had been Abe spying on him; Jake knew it wasn't the deputy, now.

Jake's hand edged towards his .45, sliding over the walnut grip. It provided him with little comfort.

A noise reached his ears: the scuffing of a foot, maybe bare, certainly not booted.

Jake whirled, whipping out the Peace-maker and swinging it in a protective arc. An empty darkened street greeted him. Tensed, he listened, waiting for the sound to come again.

Nothing.

His heart pounded in his throat, but gradually he got himself under control. Maybe he had imagined the sound.

No, he couldn't convince himself of that. He *had* heard something, but whatever it was was gone, now. He hoped.

He gave it another moment, then holstered his gun, still not confident that the menace was gone.

Maybe you're just jittery and jumping to conclusions, he told himself, sighing. He was tired, overwrought – he *could* have merely imagined it. Right?

If only he could make himself accept that.

Jake started onward again, careful not to let his boots make too much noise on the boards.

There!

Again, the gentle scuffing of a foot reached his ears. He spun, this time keeping his hand poised over his gun, but again there was nothing behind him.

Dang it! he cursed. Just calm down and wait. If whatever's out there means any harm it'll show its hand soon enough. Be ready for it!

Jake forced himself to turn and begin walking forward again, drawing on his years of experience to keep himself alert and calm at the same time. He stepped off the boardwalk and crossed in front of a deep-shadowed alley.

The sound came louder this time and he suddenly realized he was meant to hear it. Whoever stalked him was playing with him for some reason! Well, if it was a game the follower wanted, Jake would give it to him – but on *his* terms.

Jake waited, trying to pinpoint the direction from which the sound had come.

The alley. He was sure of it.

He drew his Peacemaker slowly, the full heaviness of the weapon comforting in his grip. Facing the alley, he peered into the gloom. A swatch of light bleeding from a window angled across the opposite end of the narrow throughway, and for an instant he thought he caught a glimpse of movement crossing the edge of the glow.

'You there!' Jake shouted, jutting the Peacemaker in front of him and taking a cautious step into the mouth of the alley. 'Show yourself or I'll shoot!'

Nothing.

Jake blasted a shot, not really intending to hit anything – he aimed higher than any man's head could be – but hoping to flush the varmint out.

Still nothing.

He considered trying another shot, lower,

but something suddenly slammed into him. Hard.

In a flash, he became sure the person had been playing with him all along; this time he hadn't even heard a sound as the stalker manoeuvred close enough to waylay him. Jake uttered a curse at being caught off guard, but had little time to mull it over.

A foot hit his gunhand. The Peacemaker flew off into the darkness; he heard it thud to the dirt a few feet away and knew he had no chance of retrieving it before the assailant made his next move. If the bushwhacker had a gun...

Something – a pair of arms, he realized – clamped about his waist like iron bands and hoisted him off the ground. Whoever had grabbed him possessed incredible strength. He felt himself picked clean off his feet and hurled sideways. He crashed into the ground, slamming down on his back with enough force to jolt the wind from his lungs. A groan escaped his lips – another mistake because it helped pinpoint the position of his mouth, which was promptly filled with a moccasin-clad foot.

Jake tasted hot blood filling his mouth and spat, at the same time rolling to prevent giving his attacker another clear shot. Though half-dazed, he found the move successful. He heard the bushwhacker's foot thud against the side of the building Jake had been next to a second before. Boards snapped as the foot went through.

That was Jake's chance! With the assailant's foot caught, Jake would have a split second of acting time before the stalker managed to pull himself free.

Jake heaved himself to his feet, unsteady, only the momentum of his lunge carrying him through. Making his best guess at where his foe's face would be, Jake lashed out with his fist.

He judged right!

His knuckles collided with something hard, but giving – the attacker's jaw! He heard a groan and the thud of a form hitting the ground, a beat behind the sound of a leg wrenching loose from broken wall boards.

Jake smiled to himself and pounced while he had the advantage.

The smile dropped from his face. He cursed himself for being overconfident.

A mallet-like fist hammered into his jaw and stars streaked before his eyes. He stumbled back and down, stunned. The attacker was suddenly atop him, shoving sinewed fingers into Jake's face and trying to pound the top of his skull with the other hand. Jake rolled, at the same time bringing his legs up and cross-clamping his feet about the assailant's neck. With a powerful jerk, Jake sent the attacker flying. Still unsteady, he scrambled over to the bush-whacker, fist flashing another blow.

But when Jake's fist struck, it slammed into solid ground! The attacker had moved away faster than Jake would have thought possible.

A swish of clothing told Jake the attacker was retaliating. Donovan instinctively dived sideways, but a foot thudded from his ribcage. The blow was glancing, but agony lanced his side and he suppressed a groan, not wishing to give his more-than-capable foe another opportunity.

Jake rolled. Something hard and metallic dug into the small of his back – his Peacemaker! He snatched it up and triggered a shot in front of him on reflex. Flame blasted from the muzzle; a slug tore into the opposite building. He had purposely aimed high.

A hush fell upon the alley; only the suppressed sound of labored breathing, from both Jake and his attacker, filled the darkness.

'Wait...' he heard a deep voice say after a moment.

'No tricks?' asked Jake, keeping a wary finger on the trigger.

'No tricks,' the voice responded.

Jake fumbled in his pocket for a lucifer and, finding one, struck it. Flickering flame splashed light on the area in front of him. 'What the–' he started.

'I mean you no harm,' the Indian said, folding his arms. Jake maintained his guard.

'You could have fooled me,' he said, running his tongue over his bleeding lip.

'You are mighty nervous on that.' The Indian indicated Jake's Peacemaker with a nudge of his head. 'I could not take chances.'

'Well, you almost took a bigger one than you might have lived through. I'm not crazy 'bout folks sneakin' up on me, specially in this town.' The match burned down and Jake stamped it into the dirt. 'Why don't you just move on out of the alley where I can see you plainer.'

The Indian complied, walking on to the boardwalk and standing under the dim light from a hanging kerosene lamp. Jake looked him over. The man was dressed in buckskins and moccasins, which helped explain the soundlessness with which he had moved. His face was deeply tanned and showed a weariness that seemed unnatural. Nothing about him looked particularly dangerous: in fact, he had a rather slim build, but when Jake thought of the power contained within the Indian's slight frame, he was convinced otherwise. Jake also saw the non-Indianlike Colt in the holster strapped to the man's waist. He wondered why the Indian hadn't just shot him – he had had the opportunity. Maybe the man was telling the truth about not meaning any harm.

'You'd better start explainin' fast. I've got an empty jail cell just waitin' for an occupant.'

'I came looking for you.' The Indian's voice was slow and controlled, showing no hint of intimidation.

'Well, you certainly found me. Why the attack, then?' Jake kept his Peacemaker trained on the man, not ready to trust him quite yet – and just as ready to shoot him if he made a single threatening move.

The Indian shrugged. 'Like I said, you are nervous on the trigger. I had to get your attention.'

The Indian was right, Jake conceded; he

was itchy on the trigger. With the Culverins' arrival drawing closer, he found himself more likely to draw first and ask questions later. In the back of his mind, he also knew this was one of the signs of a hired gun nearing his retirement – maybe not *over* the hill, but certainly standing at the top of it. He pushed the thought from his mind, grumbling, 'You coulda thought of a better way.'

'There was no time. I came in yesterday, though I kept myself hidden. I came looking for Luke Culverin.'

A look of surprise made its way on to Jake's face. That was the last thing he expected to hear. 'Popular bunch 'round these parts. Why do you want him?'

'I intend to kill him.'

The Indian said it in a tone that carved any glimmer of humor from the statement Jake might have found under ordinary circumstances. The thought of one man taking on the outlaws – if you took one you took them all, Jake figured – seemed ludicrous, but the Indian was dead serious.

'Plenty of men have tried – and failed. Usually they just get dead.'

'Yet you try also...'

The Indian stared directly into Jake's eyes and Jake had to admit he was right. What the Indian intended to do, Jake had also. Maybe they were both fools.

'Sometimes I don't know what's best for my own good,' he said, meaning it.

'You can put that away.' The Indian nodded towards Jake's .45. Jake studied the man's face. He was a good judge of character and right now he judged the Indian was telling the truth. If the man had wanted him dead, Jake had no doubt he would have been. Holstering the weapon, Jake kept alert to go for it if any problem arose.

'How'd you know about me?' Jake asked, curious.

'I overheard much. The people here, they are frightened, but when they are behind closed doors they talk. They said the great

Jake Donovan, *El Vengador*, had come to their town to vanquish the Culverin gang.'

Jake let out a *humph* sound, doubtful. 'They said that?'

'They have little faith you can do it.'

Any sense of ego Jake might have felt instantly deflated. The Indian had a strangely disarming manner to him. Jake reckoned the man must have quite a bit of contact with whites, because his English was better than that of most of the locals. Yet, he wasn't a breed like Jeremy Cross.

'What do you think?'

The Indian shrugged. 'I do not question a man's spirit. With it he can overcome any obstacle...'

Jake sensed a specter of sorrow haunting the man's statement. He knew suddenly that some deep pain had driven the Indian here.

'Why do you want to kill Luke Culverin? I would think an Indian would have little interest in an outlaw.'

The Indian was silent for a moment and

Jake could see a struggle going on behind his dark eyes. 'He killed my wife and daughter,' he said at last. The Indian's face remained devoid of emotion, but Jake felt the hurt, the sadness radiating from his voice. A chill shuddered down Jake's back.

'When?'

'Three years ago. My wife was a white woman. The Culverins rode through the small Wyoming town in which we lived. Luke Culverin did not think much of an Indian marrying a white woman, nor a half-breed daughter.' His voice began to quiver slightly. His eyes glossed with tears that didn't flow and Jake knew he'd had plenty of practice holding them back. 'He ... killed them, left me for dead. I think he wished to make sure I lived so I would suffer it every day of my life... He judged right. I tracked the Culverins to this town. They have left a trail of pain and destruction from here to Cheyenne. They did not think I would follow ... I would have gone on to Raco, to meet them, but I heard the talk of their return ... and you.'

Jake took the words in, feeling the Indian's pain reach out and grip him. The man had lost as much or more than the people of this town and Jake felt a deep respect for him, along with compassion. Under almost any other circumstances Jake would have thought it foolhardy to pursue the outlaws alone, but something in this man's demeanor told Jake the Indian would be more than a match for Luke Culverin alone.

'What about the others?' Jake asked, raising an eyebrow. 'They ride in together, you know. All of 'em, four, now.'

'I know. I have no particular quarrel with them, but if they get in the way...'

He let the words trail off.

'What did you want from me?'

'After I heard the talk, I judged it would be easier with two fighting. I offer my help.'

'In that case, you can make it four against four, because I've got a deputy and one feisty spitfire of a girl already on the team.'

'You will let me join you?' The Indian

160

drilled Jake with his gaze.

'Can't see why not. Judging from the way you handled yourself in the alley, the Culverins are as good as beat.'

'It will not be easy. I have seen other towns they have been through, but have always been a step behind. This time I intend to meet them.'

'Oh, you will. They're due in day after tomorrow. Can you use that thing?' Jake indicated the Colt strapped to the man's waist, knowing the question was probably stupid, but not wanting to make any assumptions.

'I can,' the Indian said simply. Jake knew he could.

Jake stuck out his hand and the Indian took it in a firm grip. 'Glad to have you aboard.'

They talked more as Jake and the Indian headed towards the Costanza Hotel. He learned the Indian's name was Joe Squatting Rock, a Crow from Wyoming who had spent a good part of his life around the white man.

His philosophy held that the white man's domination of the land was inevitable so he might as well accept the fact and live in peace with them. He also learned the Crow had no money to speak of and had slept at the edge of town with his horse the previous night. They walked to the edge of town and retrieved the animal, as well as the Indian's meager supplies, then brought the stallion to livery, Jake paying the attendant.

The Indian said he had been on the verge of approaching Jake at the hotel earlier tonight until he had seen him exit with a blonde woman and go to the hall. Jake told him about Nellie and Abe and about the preparations they had made for the Culverins' arrival. The Indian agreed quickly that he would help fight the entire gang, but made Jake promise that Luke Culverin belonged to him alone. Jake considered it a fair trade and half-pitied the Culverin brother for what might happen to him when Joe Squatting Rock avenged his family's murders.

They crossed the hotel lobby to the desk and Jeremy Cross gazed up, an irritated look on his face as he spied the Indian.

'My friend here needs a room,' said Jake, pulling out a wad of bills.

Jeremy Cross muttered something in an Indian tongue. Jake didn't understand what it was, but the tone told him it wasn't good. He looked at Joe.

'What?' Jake asked.

Joe nodded his understanding and Jake now had a fix on Cross's mix; the two were from the same area.

'He said he doesn't serve my kind here.' The expression on Joe's face didn't change. He seemed used to that type of prejudice, or resigned to it.

'Well, I'll be,' muttered Jake, sarcasm lacing his tone. 'An Indian-hating Indian!'

'I have no wish to claim my heritage,' said Cross, face bleeding red. Jake saw un-restrained anger in his dark eyes.

'I have seen your kind,' said Joe Squatting Rock softly. 'You cannot escape who you are.'

Cross looked inflamed, about to snap something at the Indian. Jake cut in, heading off any heated exchange.

'Look, mister, with the Culverins due in shortly I'm not in the frame of mind to deal with your attitude. I've about had it up to here, in fact.' Jake gestured violently with his hand at his throat. 'This man is a deputized employee and I'm telling you he'd better get a room. Understand?' Jake's temper flared and he grabbed a handful of the hotel man's shirt, yanking him close. Cross looked about to respond, but apparently, after seeing the fury in Jake's eyes, thought better of it. Jake found his nerves as tight as they would go and the proprietor had pushed him to his limit.

'I guess I don't have much choice,' muttered Cross, glancing at Joe then back to Jake. 'Won't be for long anyway.' Jake felt another surge of fury at the man's snide remark, but let it go.

'Good! Then we won't have any problems.' Jake scooped up the remaining bills and shoved them into his pocket.

'Thanks,' said Joe in a quiet voice. Jake could tell the Indian had near perfect control over his temper; that would probably be one of his strongest assets in a fight against the outlaws. Jake wished his own rage was as restrained, but maybe the Indian was just saving up his wrath for Luke Culverin.

Joe signed the book that Cross reluctantly passed to him, then they headed up the stairs. This was one night Jake thought he was actually going to get some sleep.

He was right. Falling into an exhausted slumber as soon as he hit the pillow, he dreamed of Nellie and Joe Squatting Rock and the evil leering face of Brent Culverin.

SEVEN

The next day dawned with a heat that scorched the streets of Matadero. The sun beat down with the intensity of demon fire. Heat waves danced ripply dances on the horizon as Jake arched his hand over his brow, staring down the open trail towards Raco, twenty miles away. That was the direction from which the Culverins would blast in; the oppressive temperature seemed like an omen of the hell they would bring. For a moment he could imagine their stampeding horses bounding from the wavering panorama, nostrils breathing flame and eyes blazing hellfire. He knew it was a trick of his own fear, which crawled around in his belly like scorpions, but he couldn't turn the image away.

One day.

One day until his showdown with the ruthless gang. Abe, Nellie, Joe Squatting Rock and himself – against four of the most vicious killers West Texas had ever known. How many of Jake's band would survive? He wished he could at least convince Nellie to back out, but she wouldn't hear of it. If anything happened to her...

Jake and Joe Squatting Rock had toiled the better part of the morning, preparing for the gang. Little time remained, but they had worked diligently, sweat pouring down their backs and faces, mouths parched and lips chapped. For the most part, they had boarded up more windows, nailed shut doors that weren't in immediate use and secured the most likely to be hit establishments. They had placed carts and wagons at strategic intervals and filled sacks with sand, which they then lugged to troughs they had lined up as barricades along the boardwalk near the town's opening. Jake hoped that by piling the troughs full of sacks they would have some recourse from the lead that would turn the wooden containers into kindling. His back ached from carrying the sand-filled bags, which must have weighed in excess of 150 pounds each; he had been amazed to see the Indian lugging two or three at a time. Jake had gained much respect for the Crow, finding his opinion of the man rising by the minute.

Abe had been dispatched to make sure the townspeople knew their roles – if they didn't want to fight, Jake didn't want them in the way. He was mildly surprised, however, to see a number of folk moving about freely on the street for the first time since he'd arrived. The calm before the storm? he wondered. Maybe. Nellie had decided to clean up the saloon and keep it running. She said she owed it to Ben for standing up for her. Jake reckoned she also wanted to keep busy so she wouldn't have so much time to think about tomorrow's event. He knew she had the right idea; no use dwelling on it.

Jake finished dumping a sand-filled sack

into a trough and removed his Stetson, mopping sweat from his brow with the swipe of a sleeve.

'That's the last of 'em,' he said, looking at Joe, whose face held a more emotionless look than usual. 'What's wrong?'

'That man,' said Joe, indicating a cowboy standing against a building a block down the street. The man had his hat pulled low and was busy rolling a smoke, seemingly uninterested in what was going on around him. A little too uninterested, Jake figured.

'Yeah?' Jake refitted his hat.

'He has watched us since early this morning. Do you know him?'

'No. I've seen him around, but not often 'til today. Seems harmless enough.'

'I do not know. Most people in this town ignore us. He does not.'

Jake shrugged. He couldn't figure what the man's interest could be. 'Maybe he's thinkin' of helpin' and just working at getting his courage up.'

'I do not think so.'

Jake was about to offer some other thought but held his tongue. He'd begun to have much respect for the Indian's judgement; if Joe sensed something wrong, the cowboy needed watching. They couldn't afford surprises at this late date.

The cowboy suddenly made the question moot, for the time being anyway. He finished rolling his smoke and lighting it, then without a glance in their direction sauntered off towards the Cazador. Jake saw him push through the batwing doors and disappear within.

Jake sighed. He would have to investigate that situation later.

Joe Squatting Rock scanned the street, peering at the people. 'These people care little if they get their town back,' he said without emotion.

Jake shook his head. 'They care. They're just so turn-tail scared after what's happened to 'em.' While Jake didn't much cotton to that philosophy – he'd always thought it better to face up to fear than run from it, though he s'posed technically he'd done just the opposite when he left Matadero fifteen years ago – he could tell the Indian took to it even less. After all, the Crow had lived through the Culverins' fury, had lost more than most people, but his strong spirit had forced him to battle his fear and win. He'd tracked down the Culverins, planning on facing them alone when the odds would have been overwhelmingly stacked against him.

'They show it in a peculiar way,' Joe said, leaning on the side of the trough.

Jake couldn't think of a response. The clomp-clomping of boots on the boardwalk caught his attention. Turning, he saw Abe Lincoln Hullar ambling towards them, hat in one sausage-like hand. With his free hand, the deputy was mopping his bald pate with a bandanna. The barrel-built man was perspiring freely, the front of his shirt soaked with sweat.

'Ooh, doogie!' he chirped, stepping up to Jake and Joe Squatting Rock. 'Sure is a hot one!' The deputy nodded at Joe, whom Jake had introduced to the barrel-built lawman earlier in the morning.

'How'd it go?' Jake asked.

'Most folks put up no complaint. They's just powerful afeared that this won't work and the Culverins will do them worse than they already done.'

Jake nodded, knowing the worry was genuine. A noise caught his attention and, looking down the street, he noticed a stage pulling up in front of the bank at town center. He watched for a moment, as two cowboys scrambled down from the driver's seat and hurried into the bank. Joe turned his gaze in that direction also, tiny lights twinkling in his dark eyes. The men came out a short while later, lugging sacks that they hoisted into the body of the stage. Even from the distance, Jake could see the frightened looks welded on to their faces.

'What are they doing?' Jake asked, eyeing Abe. Abe shrugged sheepishly, face almost beet red from the heat.

'Same thing they always do when the

Culverins are due in. Loadin' up the stage to send it toward Raco in the mornin'. It's sort of a ritual. The Culverins like to hit it, so they oblige.'

'What?' Jake blurted, a note of incredulity in his tone. 'They know the Culverins hit it every time yet they still send it out! That's ludicrous!'

'Yeah, whatever it were you said there. But they're too all-fired afeared not to. If they didn't, the Culverins would do even more damage.'

Joe shook his head, a hint of emotion showing on his chiselled features. Jake felt a spur of disgust dig into his gut. These people were in worse shape than he thought, if that were possible.

'Who drives it?' Jake asked, sure he wasn't going to like the answer.

'One of them will this time,' answered Abe.

'This time?'

'They hold a little lottery the night before. The loser drives the stage. Never comes back, neither, but the stage does.'

Jake could well imagine what the Culverins did with the unfortunate driver. He couldn't recall ever seeing the likes of it, a town so gripped in terror that they would willingly sacrifice one of their own for preservation of the majority.

Despite the disgust crawling through his belly, Jake began to form an idea. Maybe, just maybe, this had been what he'd been looking for, something to turn the tables. It was worth a shot, anyhow.

'Can the horses find their way to Raco alone?' he asked, glancing at Abe, then back to the men loading the stage.

'Heck, sure. They's been doin' it long enough! They could do it on their own, but that wouldn't give the Culverins no satis-faction.'

Jake nodded in slow motion. That's what he'd been hoping to hear. 'Good. Let's go down there. I just got a notion what to send on the stage to Raco – and just figured a volunteer to take it there!'

Abe looked perplexed, but the three made their way down the street to the two frightened-looking young men. Each cowboy glanced at the approaching three, but quickly went back to his work – until Jake stopped them.

'Take the sacks back into the bank and empty them,' he instructed, nodding towards the bank door. 'The Culverins won't be needin' the money and the stage won't be needin' neither of you as a driver.'

Abe's perplexed expression grew more intense and he scratched his bald head. Joe Squatting Rock stared without emotion at the proceedings. The two cowboys exchanged glances and appeared frozen.

'Go on!' snapped Jake, arching his eyebrow. 'You heard me. Do it!'

'B-but the Culverins…' stammered one of the men.

'I don't give a hoot about the Culverins! Just do what you're told or you'll have to deal with me.' The men apparently thought that over and the look Jake gave them decided it. They hurriedly gathered up the sacks and returned the cash to the bank.

'Bring the empties back out when you're done and fill them with dirt,' Jake commanded.

Abe gave Jake a bewildering look. 'What are you doin'?'

'Doing? Why I'm sending the Culverins the stage exactly the way they expect it, just with a little different payload this time.'

'Don't you think that's a mite risky?' Abe offered. Jake shrugged. 'Who do you git to drive the dang thing full of dirt? Surely not one of us!' Abe pointed to himself, Jake and Joe. 'I mean, that'd be just plain suicide, no two ways about it.'

Jake grinned and leaned a hip against the hitching rail. 'No, I have a volunteer for the job. I assure you there'll be no risk to him at all.'

Jake saw the Indian pass him a quizzical look and Abe's mouth dropped open. Jake laughed.

'There'd be a risk to–' Abe stopped, shock

welding on to his face as something seemed to dawn on him. 'You can't mean...'

'Yep, ol' Willie Culverin himself is volunteerin' for the job.' The grin on Jake's face widened and an understanding light glowed in Joe Squatting Rock's eyes. The Indian obviously approved of the plan.

'But he's dead,' Abe said.

'Which is why it won't bother him none.'

'But what's the use of sendin' it out then? Why send it at all?'

Jake laughed again. 'Well, maybe it'll buy us a bit of time, but mostly it's just for effect.'

'I cain't see it,' protested Abe, shaking his head. 'It'd only slow 'em fer an hour at the most, an make 'em madder than rattlesnakes when they see ol' Willie stiff as rawhide.'

'That's what I'm hoping. The madder they get the more likely they are to make a mistake. This might throw 'em off just a little – and that could be enough where gunfighting is concerned. I want to take away their edge. Nothing like anger to do that, eh, Joe?' Jake winked and the Indian nodded back. Jake knew the Crow's control over his temper gave him the edge over Luke Culverin. Perhaps Jake could extend it to them all by getting the gang riled up.

'I think yer jest stickin' your hand deeper into the snakepit, is all.' Abe's face twisted with disapproval.

'I have seen it work before,' put in Joe, folding his arms. 'The more calm a man's soul, the more rational his thought. I have seen men become angry in fights and lose all sense of skill. It might work.'

'It might not,' returned Abe. 'But if'n that's what you think best, I'll go along with it.'

Jake let out another laugh, the first easy emotion he'd felt since taking Nellie to the dance. The thought of irritating the Culverins held a lot of appeal to him, though he realized the plan had the potential to backfire somehow. He pushed that thought from his mind. He wouldn't let himself dwell on negative possibilities.

The two cowboys finished filling four sacks with dirt and hoisted them into the stage. While each still looked petrified, Jake also sensed each held a glimmer of relief at not having to drive the stage to the Culverins with the knowledge that he would not be returning.

After they finished loading, Jake had them take the stage away as they normally would, to ready it for going out in the morning.

Then suddenly the being watched feeling came over him again. Jake looked to Joe and the Crow nodded towards the saloon.

'He went back inside,' said Joe.

'Same guy?' asked Jake.

Joe nodded.

'I think it's time we find out what he's up to. He's taken a powerful interest in us suddenlike; I want to know why.' Jake started towards the Cazador, Joe taking up the rear, Abe staying behind. Jake had the suspicion the watcher wasn't merely gathering his courage. If a problem loomed, now was the time to deal with it.

They entered the batwing doors and Nellie waved at them from behind the bar. She had cleaned up the broken bottles and mopped up the spilled liquor. She had also refitted the splintered shelf, stocking it with what liquor was still intact. As they stepped up to the bar, she automatically poured Jake a bourbon. Joe declined a drink and took up a stool, back pressed against the bar. Jake could see Nellie had strapped a Smith & Wesson to her hip; he had no doubt that she could use it, but was half-hoping she'd change her mind.

Jake looked around the bar. He saw three men, sitting at different tables. One cowboy he had seen around town off and on; the man carried the same frightened-rabbit look that most of the townspeople sported. The man glanced at Jake, gulped the rest of the drink and headed out.

Of the other two, one was the man who'd been watching him; he had his battered hat slung about his back, his rumpled hair and unshaven face giving Jake the impression of a local hardcase. The other fellow looked more than a little familiar to Jake, though he couldn't pinpoint where he had seen him before. Somewhere in his past? Maybe. The man ignored him, except for a darted look every now and then.

Jake's attention returned to the other man, the hardcase. The man glanced up at him and Jake swore he saw a trace of a smirk. Something was up, but what?

'What's wrong?' Nellie asked, looking worried.

'That man has been watching us,' answered Joe.

'Why?' Nellie stared towards the hardcase.

Jake shrugged. 'That's what I'm about to find out.'

Jake pushed himself away from the bar and, bringing his glass, sauntered over to the man's table.

'Mind?' he asked, gesturing to a chair.

'Ain't likely to be needin' no company,' the man returned, a surly edge to his voice.

'Maybe I shouldn't have bothered askin',

then.' Jake lowered himself into a chair and slapped his glass on to the table.

'Maybe you didn't hear me right...' the man said, lips drawing into a tight line. Jake studied the man's hard eyes, sizing him up. A hardcase, all right, but of small stature. This man, Jake could tell instantly, would back down if pushed far enough. He'd seen enough of his type to know.

'Oh, I heard you plain 'nough. I'm just thinkin' you're not being very neighborly, is all.'

The man leaned forward and Jake could smell his sour breath. 'You come in here with Geronimo over there like you was some kinda saviour for this town.' Contempt laced the hardcase's tone. 'The mighty Jake Donovan, *El Vengador*. Gonna save the poor people of Matadero from the devil hisself. But maybe we don't want to be saved. Maybe we don't need yer kind of help.'

Jake stiffened, holding back his anger. 'You can think what you want, but this was once my town and I don't like what it's become.

I aim to change that. You can come along or get out...'

Jake cast the man a menacing stare. He saw a hint of backdown in the cowboy's eyes, but not much. He obviously thought he had something – or someone – to back him up.

'An' I'm tellin' you the same thing, Mr Hero. Get out right now ... while you still can.'

Jake sensed a swelling of bravado in the man's manner. Although the hardcase held some ace, Jake knew the man would never face him head on.

'I'm callin' out the Culverins tomorrow,' Jake said, leaning into the man's face. 'Nothing you can do will change that. If you get in my way you'll be sorry.'

'Is that so?'

'You can bet your life on it.' Jake stood and made his way back to the bar, draining his glass on the way. He kept the corner of his eye locked on the man just in case. The hardcase stared after him, a leer on his features, but made no threatening move.

'What's he up to?' whispered Nellie when Jake leaned on the counter.

Jake shook his head. 'Hard to tell. He's got some kinda chip that'll need watchin'. Who is he?'

'Dave Christie,' answered Nellie. 'Been in a lot of local trouble, but nothing provable. Sheriff Foreman suspected he had somethin' to do with some rustling a year back, but couldn't never pin it down. He seems to be one of the few around here who don't mind the Culverins' monthly visits.'

'Maybe he's involved with them some-how,' said Joe, turning to face them.

'Wouldn't surprise me none,' said Nellie.

'Keep an eye on him, Nell. If you even catch a glimpse of anything underhanded, tell me and I'll let him spend some time in a cell. We're too close to the gang's comin' to play games.' Jake pushed away from the bar, Joe sliding off the stool and following him.

'I'll be at the hotel if you need me,' Jake told her, then went through the doors.

EIGHT

Dave Christie swigged the last of his whiskey and muttered, 'Mr High 'n' Mighty Jake Donovan. You won't be so smart tomorrow when Brent comes ridin' in, no siree.' Dave shot a look around the bar, noticing the blonde behind the counter avert her gaze. She was a friend of Donovan and the Injun. Too bad. Dave rather fancied her, but mebbe he could get the Culverins to let him save her if'n he did 'em another favor.

Favors was what Dave was best at, wasn't it? He had acted as the gang's eyes and ears when the real outlaws weren't in town, goin' on three times, now. A real stroke of luck for him, that, gettin' in good with them hardcases. It'd been him after all who had passed Brent's messages to the gang when the outlaw was locked in Foreman's cell. And it had been him who had overheard Foreman and that no-good fat deputy talkin' 'bout hanging Brent at sun-up the next day. If not for ol' Dave, well, they might have been too late and Brent might have been swingin' from the end of the rope. They appreciated him, he reckoned.

He cast Nellie another look and sneered. Yep, that's what he wanted for the little favor he was about to do them.

Dave hoisted himself out of his chair, no easy task what with the room spinnin' and all. The liquor had gone to his head, he reckoned. He waited for things to settle in, then staggered over to the other cowboy, who was sitting alone at a back table. Lowering himself in a chair beside the man without asking, Dave slapped a hand on the table.

'You seen 'im?' Dave asked, watching the other, as he gazed up.

'I seen him.' The other took a swig of his whiskey and twisted his lips into a disgusted grimace.

'He's plannin' on takin' away the best thing that ever happened to this town.'

The other let out a *pfft* sound. 'The Culverins? Can't rightly say they been any help to this dump. The only ones ever to put a dang into this town was the Cardonas, and they're all gone.'

Dave smiled, his vision clouding a moment then coming back into focus. 'No, yer wrong. The Culverins can be real generouslike – if'n you help them out.'

'Like you been doin'?' the other asked sarcastically.

'That's dang right! Like I been doin'.' The snide remark went past Dave; he thought he was getting somewhere.

'Frankly, I don't give a hoot what happens to this God-forsaken hole. When the Culverins come in, Donovan will get what's comin' to him. Who cares if he takes out a couple of them outlaws along the way?'

'You do,' answered Dave, ignoring the remark and waving his hand.

'I do?' The other man stared at Dave, his

gaze dulled by whiskey.

'Donovan kilt your friend, Miguel, remember?'

'I remember. Not likely somethin' I'd fergit.'

'Well, now he plans to do the same to the Culverins, but we ain't gonna let him.'

'We ain't?'

'No, you gotta avenge poor Miguel's death. You gotta call Donovan out!' Dave slapped the table again and the glass of whiskey jumped.

The man gave Dave a look he couldn't read, but Dave could tell he'd struck a nerve. 'Sure,' Dave continued. 'And if you take care of Donovan, well, then, the Culverins will be real kindly to you for that. I know 'em. They got honor.' Dave didn't bother to tell the man he planned to take most of the credit, maybe all. He had seen this cowboy shoot and knew if anyone had a chance – and a reason – to beat Donovan, this cowboy did.

'I don't know...' the man said. His words

had acquired a touch of whiskey slur, and Dave reckoned that would make his task all the easier.

'Look, I'll be there to back you up. You have to call him out. It's the only right thing to do!'

'What in tarnation would you know about right?' the man spat back. 'You're in with them.'

'That's why I know what I'm talkin' about. Don't you remember what that sidewinder did to Miguel? How he left him dyin' in the street like a no-good? Don't you remember how the old man took his boy's death?'

'Yes, I remember. Diego wasn't never the same after that. I wasn't, neither.'

'The Cardonas made this town what it is. How can you let Miguel's death pass? Now's your chance at the man who took it all away. You got no choice ... and I can make sure the Culverins appreciate it.'

The cowboy seemed to consider it, a mixture of drunk bravado and fear dancing in his eyes. Dave could see the man wavering and knew he almost had him.

'Look, see that little filly over yonder?' He nudged his head towards the bar, where Nellie was keeping a sideways eye on them. The cowboy nodded.

'Well, you know what Miguel thought about her. They was gonna get hitched an' all. The old man had it arranged.'

'I remember. Miguel had his sights set on her in a powerful way. He hated Donovan for coming between them.'

'That's right.' Dave decided it was time to drive the point home. 'Donovan hurt her, too, when he killed Miguel in cold blood. It destroyed her life; she ain't never got hitched since.' The other nodded his understanding. 'And I think you could have her if you got Donovan out of the way. He's back for her, you know. He's got his eye set on her and she'll have no chance.'

'You think she'd go for me?' the other asked, eyes narrowed.

'I know it! Miguel would want it that way. You was his best friend.'

'Yeah...' said the other, downing the last of his glass. 'Yeah, you're right, he would!' The man sprang up, kicking his chair over backward. He slammed a fist on the table. 'You're right! That no-good killer's gotta pay. I shoulda done it when I first laid eyes on him!'

Dave saw Nellie cast them a look and concealed a grin. 'He's at the Costanza with that Injun pal of his.' The man nodded forcefully and, sliding fingers over his Colt, stalked from the saloon. Behind him, Dave let a wide grin spread over his lips. He shoved back his chair and gained his feet.

Looking at Nellie, an evil leer on his features, he said, 'Your friend came back to the wrong town, missy. He shoulda stayed away, let things be.'

'What do you mean?' Nellie asked. He could hear the nervousness in her voice and liked it. Yep, he would make sure the Culverins knew what he had done for them and gave her to him. He laughed and slammed aside the batwings, going out into the bright sunlight. He wanted to be around when the mighty Jake Donovan went down.

Jake lay stretched out on the bed, finding himself wishing the day would pass more quickly. The waiting, he reckoned, was the hardest part. Early tomorrow, he would send the stage out, thereby sending the Culverins a message that would, he hoped, signal an end to their reign of fear over this town. After the stage departed, again they would wait. Abe said the Culverins always came in about noon. Jake reckoned that was OK: there wasn't much else they could do in the way of protection anyway.

Jake had hoped he could get some more rest before tomorrow dawned. He would need all his strength and guile, so he wanted to be well slept, or at least as relaxed as he could be given the circumstances.

A voice snapped his reverie, one that ended any thought of sleep. Jake tensed. He swung his feet out of bed. Pulling on his boots, he felt his heart begin to thump. The voice came again, calling his name from the street. Jake didn't like the tone of it one bit.

Going to the window, Jake peered out. In the street below, poised in an offensive stance, hands inches above his guns, stood the familiar-looking cowboy Jake had seen in the Costanza. Again the thought that he knew the man from somewhere struck him, and again he couldn't pin it down.

'What the–' he mumbled.

The man yelled, 'I'm callin' you out, Jake Donovan! Come out here and face me, you yella-belly!'

A chill rattled down Jake's back. He understood the threat that confronted him, though he couldn't guess why. He considered ignoring it; he didn't need this right now. His thoughts immediately swung to the other man in the saloon, the hardcase, Dave Christie. He bet the no-good had something to do with this.

For an instant, Jake had taken his eyes off the man in the street, which proved a mistake. A rock crashed through the window, shattering the pane and spraying Jake with shards. Jake leaped back, cursing, knowing he now had little choice but to face the challenge unless he could somehow talk the other man out of it. But until he could fathom a reason for the other man calling him out, there was little chance of that.

Jake strapped on his gunbelt in haste, pulled his Peacemaker out, put it in, pulled it out, put it in again, making sure the feel was right. Going to his door, he pulled it open. Joe Squatting Rock stood in the hall, waiting for him. The Indian had the room next door and had surely heard what transpired.

'Trouble,' said Jake and the Indian nodded, following him along the dingy corridor and down the stairs. Jeremy Cross was behind the desk and gave them his usual disparaging look.

'Maybe I'll get rid of you early,' he said, turning and going into the back room. Jake's anger boiled but he didn't have time for the hotel man right now.

The front doors burst open and Nellie came flying through, a worried look on her face.

'Jake, don't! Dave Christie riled that feller up somehow. He aims to kill you!'

'So I gathered,' said Jake through tight lips. 'Who in tarnation is he?'

'He was a friend of Miguel's...'

That was all Nellie needed to say. Jake remembered in a flash where he had seen the man before. He was constantly by the young Cardona's side fifteen years ago, and like a second son to the old man. Jake cursed himself for not being quicker to remember. Perhaps it could have meant avoiding the present predicament. Then again, perhaps it wouldn't have mattered anyway; some circles just had a way of closing.

'I have to go, Nell. Stay in here.'

'No, I'm coming!'

Jake knew he couldn't change her mind. He turned to Joe Squatting Rock, who was looking past him to the street.

'There is no reason to face this man. There

197

is too much to risk. If you lose...'

Jake considered it. The Indian had the better argument, but Jake couldn't dismiss the code he'd lived under for fifteen years. The problem had to be dealt with now, though he knew the outcome might not be one he desired. If it were let go, it might hinder their plan against the Culverins tomorrow. But now at least Jake had a clue to the man's motive; if he could use that...

'I have to go. I can't take the chance of it causing problems later.' Jake walked through the doors into the stinging sunlight, allowing a moment for his eyes to adjust to the glare.

'Jake Donovan, you lily-livered coward!' snapped the man. 'You shot Miguel in cold blood. I have come to avenge him!' The cowboy stood rigid, hands poised above his guns.

Jake felt his stomach sink, noting the man was half-drunk and knowing that would make reasoning with him all the more unlikely.

'Look, son, I didn't kill Miguel in cold blood. He bushwhacked me–'

'That's a lie!' the man screamed. Jake saw the cowboy's temper had been wound up to a blind fury. 'You killed him because you wanted his woman. Now I want her and I want peace for Miguel!' The man jutted a finger towards Nellie, who had stepped out on to the boardwalk.

'Please listen to reason,' Jake pleaded. 'It's been fifteen years. It's time to let the past rest–'

'No! For Miguel there is no rest unless you are dead!'

Jake saw it start. He knew there was no turning back, now. The man's eyes had given it away, followed almost a split second later by a jerk of his hands towards his guns.

Jake had no choice; he went for his Peacemaker.

The cowboy's Colts flashed out and Jake was almost caught off guard by the man's speed, especially given his drunken condition. But Jake pulled a half-second faster.

His Peacemaker shot up, levered, boomed!

The man jerked backwards, still managing to squeeze off a shot that plowed into the ground inches in front of Jake's boots.

Jake got his second surprise then. For one of the few times in his life he had misjudged his shot. The cowboy stopped his backward stumble, jerked the gun up for another shot. The bullet had hit his chest, but not where Jake had intended it to, his heart, which would have brought instant death. The man fired and Jake dived. Where Donovan had been, a slug tore into the dirt.

Jake tumbled sideways, came up on a knee, hand fanning the hammer of his Peacemaker. Three slugs slammed into the cowboy's frame, kicking him back and down. His body crashed into the dust, lay still.

Jake's heart pounded as he gained his feet, adrenalin surging through his veins and nausea rising in his belly.

He edged over to the body, a feeling of heavy sadness settling over him. From the corner of his eye, he caught the movement of someone slipping around the side of a building into the alley; Dave Christie, come to see the results of his dirty work, Jake guessed. Results the hardcase had not wanted.

He crouched over the fallen gunfighter, saw that the cowboy was indeed dead. Nellie and Joe came up behind Jake, Nellie laying a hand on his shoulder. Abe came running up from down the street.

'What happened?' he stammered, out of breath, face a mask of worry and concern.

'Give this man a decent burial,' Jake said, ignoring the question and standing.

'Jake, there was nothing you could do,' ventured Nellie, sympathy in her tone.

'Wasn't there?' he returned, hating the feeling in his soul. 'I'm tired of this happening, Nell. Everywhere I go, everywhere I've been it's the same. It hasn't stopped since I left, fifteen years ago.'

'It's over, Jake. This was the last tie to the Cardonas. You can relax now.'

'No, I can't. Not with the Culverins coming in tomorrow. Even then, I wonder, will it ever be over?' He sighed a deep tortured sigh and turned to Abe. 'After you've finished, round up Dave Christie. That no-good is going to have to answer for this and I don't want him runnin' loose when the Culverins show up.' Abe nodded.

Jake walked towards the hotel, Nellie accompanying him, her arm in his. Joe Squatting Rock helped Abe haul the dead man to a wagon.

Leaving Nellie at the door, Jake headed up to his room, preferring solitude for the rest of the day. He knew there would be no sleep tonight. And now he knew tomorrow would come only too fast...

NINE

When the sun rose the next day, Jake Donovan climbed out of bed and yawned. Apprehension twisted like snakes in his belly and he hadn't slept a wink all night. His mind had been too cluttered with thoughts of the Culverins, Nellie and of the things that had plagued him for the last fifteen years. Only now, after a sleepless night of asking questions of himself, he thought he might have found some answers. But those would have to wait until after his showdown with the outlaws.

Sunlight slanted dusty rays through the window and fell across the floorboards in wedge-like patterns. He hadn't bothered to fix the window pane; the night had been relatively warm and with the sunrise the room had become downright stifling.

Jake strapped on his Bowie knife and gunbelt, first checking the Peacemaker and his supply of ammunition.

'For something I don't like usin', you're sure gettin' your fill of work lately,' he muttered, holstering the .45. 'Let's hope today will bring an end to it.'

Donovan wished he could assure himself it would.

Jake stepped out into the hall and went to the next room, knocking hard to roust Joe Squatting Rock. The Indian answered immediately and Jake was quite sure he hadn't slept that night either. The Crow gave him his typical expressionless look and Jake put a hand on his shoulder. 'Whatever happens today,' he said with a trace of a smile, 'I just want you to know I'm a better man countin' you as a friend.' He offered a callused hand and the Indian took it, nodding. Jake knew the Crow felt the same way.

They made their way down the stairs and Jake was surprised to see Jeremy Cross was strangely absent.

'Huh,' Jake muttered. 'Wonder what that sidewinder's up to. I'd have thought he'd be itchin' to put in his two cents today.'

Joe Squatting Rock shrugged. 'Perhaps he is hiding. That seems to be his nature.'

Jake chuckled as they left the hotel, walking to the saloon. Jake breathed in deep gulps of early morning air, which was refreshing despite its warmth.

They found Nellie already in the saloon. Sitting themselves at the table, Jake gave her a warm smile when she brought over a pot of steaming coffee and filled the cups she set in front of them. They drank in silence, feeling the heat strengthen and become oppressive as the sun angled its way higher in the sky. An hour later, Abe wandered in, rubbing his eyes and yawning. He obviously had gotten some sleep, but his face looked drawn and pale. As he set his battered hat on the table and lowered his bulk into a chair, pouring himself a cup of brew after locating a tin cup behind the bar, he rubbed his bald head and let out a long sigh.

'I don't mind a'tellin' ya, I got a case of the flutters in my belly big enough to kill a mule. I ain't lookin' forward to this.'

'None of us are, Abe,' said Nellie, sipping from her cup. 'But it has to be done.'

Jake nodded and said, 'The stage all set?'

'Pretty much. Just gotta round up ol' Willie and give him the reins. Better hope they find 'im quicklike 'cause he ain't gonna be smellin' so good after the hot sun hits him for a spell.'

Jake didn't want to think about that and pushed the notion from his mind. 'Everything else is ready except the saloon. Abe will help you board it, Nell – there's no way I can talk you out of this?'

Nellie shook her head. A look of resolve welded on to her features. 'Not on your life. We'll board up the door and I'll take out the window so I can shoot. Reckon I can hit them from here easy with that 30-30 you gave me, and if they get any closer...' She patted the shooter on her hip.

'Joe and I will meet them head on and give them one chance to surrender,' Jake said. The Crow glanced at him, a flicker of disapproval crossing his face, but held his tongue. Jake knew the Crow would just as soon deal with the gang with lead, and Jake doubted he could stop the Indian if he decided to put a slug into Luke. But he found he really didn't care. Giving the gang a chance to surrender was most likely a moot point; he knew they wouldn't, but had to try. He would let them choose their own fate.

'Any sign of Dave Christie?' Jake asked Abe, finishing his coffee.

'Not a hide. He musta high-tailed it.'

'I wonder...' mused Jake.

'What's he got to stick around for?' Abe's eyes narrowed, almost disappearing into the deep pockets of flesh surrounding them.

'Let's just hope he didn't go off to warn the Culverins.'

An hour later found Jake and Joe Squatting Rock at the stage, propping an uncooperative, not to mention dead Willie Culverin into the driver's seat. Abe had remained behind to help Nellie board up the Cazador, agreeing to meet Jake and Joe at the mouth of town at 11.30. That would give them nearly an hour and a half to get themselves ready.

While Joe held the dead outlaw in place, Jake finished tying him to the seat. He tightened the ropes; he didn't want Willie tumbling out during the ride and spoiling things.

'Let's hope this puts a burr in their britches,' said Jake grabbing the reins and turning the horses. He led the animals down the street to the edge of the hard-packed trail. 'Well, here goes nothin'.' He yelled, putting the stage into motion. The horses charged forward, instinctively knowing the path, and bounded down the trail towards Raco. Jake and Joe watched them disappear in a cloud of dust.

Brent 'Smiley' Culverin let out a drunken

whoop and shot out of the window of the Do-right Eatery. He pounded a fist on the table and yelled for the waitress, a timid auburn-haired girl who tentatively edged up to the table. The Culverin brothers laughed at the girl's fright-filled expression. They'd been up all night, getting a head start on what was left of Raco's whiskey supply, then had come over to the eatery for breakfast.

The girl drew close and Brent snapped a hand out, grabbing her. She let out a mew and he chuckled. Oh, how he liked the smell of fear, especially from a woman. 'This bacon here ain't cooked right, honey,' he said, a piece of egg clinging to the side of his stubbly face. The scar wiggled repulsively. 'Maybe you could make it right for me...' He pursed his lips to give the girl a kiss, yanking her close. She struggled and tears began to roll down her face. Brent heaved her back. He hated girls who cried. Wasn't even worth his time. Willie on the other hand... Say, where in tarnation was Willie anyhow? He had ridden out early the other day and Brent hadn't seen a lick of him since. Usually Willie came back within the next day or two.

The other Culverins guffawed at the waitress as she stumbled off, blubbering.

'You were a mite hard on the filly, weren't you, Brent?' Mace asked sarcastically. The ugly half-grin spread over Brent's features and he swiped his hand over his mouth, knocking the fleck of egg loose. They all chuckled.

Then Brent's face turned serious. 'We been in this dump long enough. They got better women in Matadero – and better food!' His hand lashed out, knocking his plate to the floor with a loud clatter. The plate shattered, bacon, eggs and homefries splattering across the boards.

'Time we found out what your no-good brother is up to anyhow,' he added. Brent stood, heading for the door, the other Culverins trailing after him. 'Stage will be about due, now...'

He mounted his roan. 'Wouldn't want to

disappoint the good people of Matadero by missing it, would we?' He grinned, the scar wriggling like a white snake in the sunlight. 'Let's give this dung-heap somethin' to remember us by, boys!' He yanked out his Colt and began to shoot, his horse neighing and rearing. His duster flew behind him as the horse bolted forward. Townspeople, the few out and about, scurried as the brothers took shots at windows and troughs, punching holes in the wooden containers so that water spewed out in long streams.

They rode the length of Raco, horses' hooves thundering, guns blazing, then out on to the hard-packed trail that wound towards Matadero.

Ten miles on, Brent slowed his horse, brothers following suit. In the distance, he could see the dim shape of the approaching stage, a speck trailed by billowing dust.

'There it is, boys! Right on schedule.' Brent smiled, thinking how much he liked this game. It reminded him of the times years back when he used to raid Crow camps and shoot the peaceful Indians just for the fun of it.

The brothers pulled their bandannas over their lower faces; it was part of the ritual.

'Yee-hah!' shouted Brent, charging his horse forward. They rode hard for ten minutes, a cyclone of beating hooves and whooping men. As the stage drew near, they began to shoot in the air, the signal for the driver to begin slowing the careening animals.

Something was wrong. Brent sensed it immediately. The stage hadn't missed a beat!

Brent slowed his horse. 'Why that no-good driver!' he yelled.

'He ain't gonna stop!' shouted Mace, jabbing a finger towards the stage, which was cutting the distance between them with startling rapidity. If they didn't move out of the way, Brent thought the danged thing might actually run them down. Of all the gall-darned nerve...

'I can see that, you half-breed!' he yelled at

Mace. 'Well, we'll just have to stop it then. If they want to play hard, we'll teach 'em a lesson!' Brent felt anger boil in his veins. Yes, a lesson was well in order. Nobody resisted the Culverins. Nobody!

They drove their horses into motion, spreading out in an effort to surround the approaching stage. Brent managed to work his way around the chariot as it thundered past, then charged up alongside. He leaned over in his saddle, yelling, made a grab at the reins, which were flying loose. He didn't have time to give the driver a second look, but he'd deal with the skunk as soon as he got the stage stopped. Mace bolted up on the other side and lent a hand. Within a few moments they got the charging team slowed, then stopped.

The Culverins edged around the stage, two on each side, guns drawn. 'Hey you!' Brent yelled at the driver, whose head was slumped against his chest. 'What do you think you're pullin'?'

'Hey,' said Mace, a startled look on his

face. 'That's Willie!'

Brent peered closer, shielding his eyes against the sun with an arched hand over his brow. It *was* Willie! What the–

'Willie, what do you think you're doin'?' he asked in an irritated tone, climbing down from his horse. He went up to the stage and halted, tugging at the driver's duster. 'Hey, he's all trussed–' Brent stopped. He had spotted the stiffness to his brother's form. His gaze fell to the brown patch that stained half his brother's shirt, then to the burnt hole square over his heart. The heated breeze brought the stench of death into his nostrils.

'Nooo!' he screamed, balling his fists. A thunder commenced in his head, threatening to split his skull wide open. The thunder of anger, rage, fury! 'Who did this?' he continued screaming. *'Who did this?'* The other brothers drew back, not wanting to be within striking distance when the fever came over him. Brent pounded a fist at the side of the stage, fury sending his blow clear through the weak construction. He tore the

ropes from Willie's body and lowered his youngest brother to the ground. For the first time in years, something close to sorrow filled his body. Then anger flooded back in, but now it was directed, controlled and ready to strike.

'I want the bastard who did this to Willie! That whole town will pay for this!'

'Brent, maybe we oughta think twice about goin' into Matadero,' offered Mace, shaking his head. 'Somethin's up.'

'You're danged right something's up!' Brent screamed back. 'Don't get lily-livered on me, now!' He drilled Mace with his black-steel eyes and Mace recoiled visibly, shutting his mouth.

'Someone's a'comin'!' Luke blurted, pointing. Down the trail, they saw a rider storming towards them. Jake drew his Colt and mounted his roan. The Culverins sidled up beside their leader and waited for the approaching horseman.

'It's that idiot, Dave Christie,' said Brent, eyeing the rider, who stopped his bay before them. The brothers gathered close and Dave's face took on a worried look. Brent drew up beside him.

'What is this...?' he asked in a dead tone.

'They got the town ready for you, Brent,' Christie stammered. 'I seen 'em making preparations. They mean to kill you all. I tried to stop—'

'*Who?*' Brent snapped, teeth clenched.

'Jake Donovan. He's got an Injun and that fat deputy, Hullar, with him. They intend to take back their town.'

Brent shook his head. He had never heard of Jake Donovan and couldn't imagine why the man would dare oppose them. Then he glanced at his brothers, searching their faces for any recognition of the name.

'I heared of him,' Loomis said. 'Saw him in a town I was in once. A hired gun, a bad *hombre*. They call him the Avenger from Matadero. He musta come back.'

Dave nodded, rabbitlike. 'He made himself sheriff after Hullar told him what was going on in the town. It was Donovan who kilt Willie.'

Brent's face twisted with rage. 'What are they doing?'

Dave gave Brent the details, telling him how they had secured the opening of the town to meet the incoming gang.

Brent spat. 'Well, we'll just have to accommodate Mr Donovan, won't we boys?' He glanced around; none of the brothers voiced an objection.

'You did good, Dave,' said Brent in an all-too-cool tone. 'Now, what do you want?'

Dave grinned. 'There's that Cantrell gal... She's been running the saloon and Donovan has latched on to her. After you kill him...'

A leer slid on to Brent's face. 'She's yours.'

'Maybe a reward, too?' Dave ventured. 'I been kinda down on my luck lately.'

Brent's leer widened. 'Sure, Dave, you can have your reward.'

Dave smiled eagerly.

'As a matter of fact, I got some spare cash right here.' Brent's hand lashed to his Colt, whipping it loose and levering it.

'Brent, no, I did what you wanted! I warned you!' The man's face twisted with terror at the sight of the outlaw's aimed Colt.

'Yeah, but you see, I'm all-fired angry right now at losing Willie there. I just gotta get rid of some of it!' Brent fired.

Dave Christie flew off his horse, a bullet between the eyes. Slamming into the ground, he lay still.

'Why'd you do that, Brent?' asked Mace. 'He might have still been useful.'

Brent shrugged. 'He's more useful this way. Besides, after I get through with Matadero, we won't have no reason to ever go back.' He let his words sink in a moment. 'Loomis, give your brother a decent burial over yonder. Mace, you and Luke put Dave into the stage and turn it around. We're gonna give Mr Jake Donovan, whoever the hell he thinks he is, a taste of his own medicine – lead medicine!'

'You gotta plan?' asked Luke, smiling.

'I gotta plan.'

TEN

Nellie Cantrell kneeled and stared out into the street through the busted-out pane in the window. She glanced at the Winchester propped against the wall, ready to lever it into action as soon as she caught sight of the Culverins. She couldn't deny the fluttering of anticipation and nerves in her belly. Her anticipation came from the hope that the threat looming over Matadero would finally be ended, but her nervousness – the stronger of the feelings – didn't come from fear of the outlaws. It came from fear of what might happen to Jake. She knew their chance against the gang was about as good as her chance of getting Jake to the altar. Even with the odds even, four against four, she had grave doubts. Abe wasn't a crack shot by any means, and she was holed up

219

behind the boarded-up doors of the saloon. Jake and Joe Squatting Rock would take the brunt of the attack on the front lines, so essentially it would be two against the outlaws. She forced the thought from her mind; she couldn't let it cloud her judgement 'cause Jake needed her, now. If they came through this and Jake left again, at least she'd have a fleeting moment of satisfaction for their renewed time together.

'Dang it, Jake Donovan, you'd better come out of this alive or I'll kill you myself!' She took a deep breath and tried to laugh at her own joke, but found her humor in bad repair.

The sudden scuff of a boot behind her sent a wave of chills down her back. She froze, then slowly let out the breath jammed in her lungs. She began to edge around, stopping short as the cold muzzle of a gun dug into her neck.

'Turn around, slowlike,' a harsh voice commanded. She complied as the muzzle drew back. She turned to face the sneering features of Brent Culverin and a rush of coldness shuddered through her being. Her gaze shifted to the Winchester only a couple of feet from her hand, then quickly back to the outlaw. She calculated her chances of getting to the weapon, but knew she'd be dead before she got within inches of it.

'That's right, little lady, don't even think of it!' Brent's black-eyes bored into her like daggers from beneath his battered hat. 'You'd be dead before you could twitch.'

'What do you want?' Nellie asked, forcing her voice to remain as steady as it would given the circumstances.

'Want? Why nothin' – 'cept this here town and your Mr Donovan. See, I heared he killed Willie, and I ain't likely to forgive him for that anytime soon.'

'Jake'll kill you.'

'Will he now?' Brent let out a harsh laugh. 'That's funny, little lady, real funny. That idiot Dave Christie was right: you got a hankerin' for Donovan, doncha? Well, I can see what he sees in you.' Brent let his gaze wander the length of her form with appreciation. 'I just might save y'all for myself. Now get up!'

Nellie did as she was told, rising slowly until she was standing. She considered screaming to warn Jake but knew she would be dead before he could hear her.

Brent gestured towards her waist. 'Drop that.'

Nellie unbuckled her gunbelt and let it fall to the floor. Brent motioned her over to a table, making her take a seat. She sat on the edge, alert for any chance to escape.

'What're you gonna do?' she asked, wanting to keep his attention diverted in case Jake or Squatting Rock got the notion to come back and check on her, though she doubted they would.

'Don't you worry that pretty little head of your'n over that. You'll learn soon 'nough. Until then, maybe you and I can spend some time together...'

Brent laughed and started towards her.

Abraham Lincoln Hullar ambled around the corner into an alley that bisected Main Street and a back avenue. He gave his drooping britches a hitch and tucked in his shirt, patting his ample belly. He pulled out his gun as he walked, absently checking the cylinders. He halted, and, satisfied he was ready, snapped the chamber shut. 'Jeez, I sure hope ol' Jake knows what he's doin'.' He mopped sweat from his brow. He wasn't too all-fired sure 'bout that stage trick. What if it backfired and made Brent Culverin and his boys all the madder? Abe had seen the gang in action more times than he cared to count, and he had no desire to see them all roared up. Abe spat, pulling up his hat and running his bandanna over his bald pate. He replaced the hat and stood in the alley, one hand on his hip, the other still clenching his six-shooter, contemplating first the Culverins, then Donovan and the Indian. His mind went to Miss Nellie at the saloon. Jake told Abe to check and make sure she was safely holed up in the saloon. He didn't want anything to happen to her. Abe might not have been around to prevent what happened to Sheriff Foreman, but he vowed he'd fight to his dyin' breath this time to make sure nothing hurt Miss Nellie.

The click of a hammer being drawn back jerked Abe from his thoughts. He froze where he stood. A shudder worked its way down his spine and he felt a stream of sweat trickle down his face.

'Well, well,' came a voice from behind him. 'I didn't rightly believe it when Christie said you was hangin' around, fat boy, but I guess he wasn't lyin'.'

Abe recognized the voice and a bolt of horror sizzled through him. One of the Culverins, he was sure. He glanced down, careful not to move his head, eyed the six-shooter in his hand. His hand bleached as his grip tightened on the weapon. He wasn't a fast shot; he knew it. But did the Culverin know the gun was in his hand?

'Go ahead, Deputy. Try a shot. You jest might get lucky.'

That settled that, Abe thought with a note of panic. The outlaw knew about the gun. Abe reckoned he had little choice, now. If he spun and tried a shot, the outlaw would gun him down sure. But if he didn't, the hardcase would shoot him in the back.

Some choice, he told himself.

'Whatcha want?' Abe tried, hoping to keep the Culverin off guard.

'Want?' the outlaw mocked. 'Why you dead, of course–'

Abe spun. He had no other option with the outlaw's words. As sure as he was standing there, he knew the brother was levelling his gun and inching the trigger in for a shot that would come any second.

Abe got half-around before he felt a burning welt of agony rip into his shoulder, the boom of a Colt a split second before.

Abe reeled, off balance as the slug plowed into his flesh. He felt the left side of his upper body go numb. He managed to turn fully. He saw Loomis Culverin grinning like something from a nightmare. Abe felt blood pour down his back. He knew the wound wasn't fatal, but the next one would be.

The brother laughed, aimed for another shot. Abe called on every last ounce of strength he had. Swinging his gun up, he jerked the trigger. A shot blasted, echoing from the building walls. A look of shock flittered on Loomis's face as the slug tore into his chest. He staggered backward a step, disbelief like the face of Death in his eyes. He looped his gun up. With dying fingers he triggered a final shot.

Lead burned into Abe's belly and a pool of blood spread across his shirt. He stumbled back, crashing into a wall. As he crumbled to the ground, blood dribbling from his mouth, a sense of satisfaction forced his lips into a weak smile. He saw the Culverin brother crumple into a heap on the dirt, unmoving. Abe knew his shot had been true, even if death had come a mite off schedule.

Abe sat against the building, his breath rumbly and labored. He knew he was dying, but it didn't matter. He hadn't let Jake down.

'I done you proud, Frank...' he muttered, blood bubbling from his lips. 'Miss ... Nellie...' Abe fought to stave off the blackness pulling at his mind. He tried to move, to keep alive, knowing there was nothing he could do as his lifeblood flowed from the hole in his belly...

'Something's gone wrong,' said Joe Squatting Rock from his crouched position near Jake Donovan at the outskirts of Matadero.

'What makes you say that?' asked Jake, feeling the same way but reluctant to voice it.

'The deputy should have been here by now.'

'I told him to check on Nellie, but he should have been back by now. Maybe he got hung up with something.' Even as Jake said it he knew it wasn't the case. Something *had* gone wrong, but what?

The problem became suddenly irrelevant

as the Indian jutted a finger towards the open trail. 'The stage is coming back.' Joe's voice carried no emotion, but a look of vague worry played in his dark eyes.

Jake's heart jumped to his throat. In the distance he could see the stage thundering towards the town, the rattling clamor of its wheels and the animals' hooves echoing louder and louder. It confirmed their suspicions of something amiss; the stage wouldn't be coming back unless something had gone terribly wrong.

'Let it come, there's no driver,' said Jake. He moved to one side of the street and Joe crouch-walked to the other, gun drawn.

The stage careened towards them, devouring the distance in less than two minutes. Jake prepared himself, intending to stop it. He had to make sure his timing was just right, or he risked being trampled beneath the animals' beating hooves.

He leaped on to the lip of one of the sandbag-filled troughs to get some height. The stage drew closer, closer, closer. Only a few feet, now; ten – five – three – one–

Jake leaped into space as the team hurled past! With a bone-jarring jolt he thudded against the lead horse, grabbing the harness and struggling to get himself atop the animal. His boot snagged a brace, giving him a bad moment, but he yanked his foot loose and pulled himself up from his position dangling on the side. Sweat poured from his forehead. Every muscle screamed with every hard-fought inch he gained. Finally, he topped the stallion, then worked his way back to the driver's seat and grabbed the reins. He yanked back hard and the animals slowed, not frightened, merely unguided. He forced them to stop and Joe Squatting Rock came trotting up beside the stage. Jake hopped down, his breath rasping out, his frame soaked with sweat and his muscles quivering from the effort.

They examined the stage and Jake pulled the door open. The blood-soaked body of Dave Christie flopped into the street with a thud. Jake peered at the Indian, face tense.

'Our little ruse failed,' Jake said panting. 'They sent it back on us.'

'Maybe,' said the Indian. 'But maybe it made them just mad enough to make a mistake.'

'I have my doubts–'

Shots boomed from an alley and Jake stiffened, jerking his head in that direction. 'What the–'

More shots, this time from the distance. Then the encroaching thunder of hooves.

'They are coming,' said Joe, unlimbering his gun again.

'Yaah!' Jake shouted, sending the horses on down the street. He knew it would alert Nellie of the Culverins' approach.

Jake and Joe ran back towards the outskirts and scrambled into position. They could see horses riding in at full gallop from a mile down the trail.

'There's only two of 'em!' said Jake. That he didn't like one bit. Remembering the shots he had heard a moment ago from the alley, he liked it even less.

The Indian nodded. 'There will be no taking them alive. Do not risk your life trying.'

Jake found himself forced to agree. All bets were off. Two Culverins were storming in from the south, but that left two unaccounted for. If they had already snuck in—

'Watch your back,' he told Joe Squatting Rock. 'They could have sent in two early.' Jake cursed his idea of sending the stage out, but didn't have long to dwell on it.

Taking up defensive positions, Jake behind a sandbag-filled trough and Joe behind a barrel, also filled with sand, they waited.

But not long.

The two Culverins charged in, guns blazing. Lead gouged dirt from the street and splintered wood from buildings. Jake pumped a shot in their direction and one of the brothers' horses reared, beating the air with its hooves, almost spilling the outlaw. The hardcase fought the reins and brought the horse under control. The gang split up, each dismounting and zig-zagging off to either side. Jake got a glimpse of the outlaws' faces, seeing the leader was missing. He didn't see Loomis, either, so the two had to be Luke and Mace.

A hush fell over the street as the Culverins took over.

Jake glanced at Squatting Rock. 'Which one is Luke?'

'The one on the right,' the Crow answered. Jake could see the intensity in his eyes as the Indian stared in the direction the outlaw had taken.

'You got 'im! That leaves me Mace.' Jake saw Joe edge forward, then bolt, blasting shots in the direction of the brother he wanted. Jake suddenly drew his head back as a slug plowed into the trough protecting him. Splinters struck his face but did no damage. The sandbags had stopped the bullet from coming through and Jake was thankful for at least that small piece of planning.

'Give yourself up!' he yelled, knowing

there was no chance of it.

A harsh laugh thundered back.

'Go to Hades, lawman, or whatever you call yourself now, Donovan!'

That would be Mace, the brains of the outfit, Jake told himself. A shot cracked in the distance. Jake couldn't tell if it came from Joe or Luke's gun.

Leaping from cover, Jake darted in a half-crouch along the boardwalk, triggering lead in front of him. Mace's gun ripped back and numerous shots came closer than Jake found comfortable. He managed, however, to draw a general location on the brother. Mace was holed up to the left, behind an empty wagon. Doubling over and coming up behind a barrel, Jake could see the gunman's boots in the gap between wagon and ground. He bolted into the street, firing a round into the wagon above where the boots stood. As the slug tore through the brittle wood, the boots didn't move and Jake let out a violent curse, instantly realizing he'd fallen for a trick. A grating laugh echoed out and the brother sprang from the end of the wagon, levelling his Colt. The outlaw had used the few seconds in which Jake's attention had been diverted to haul out of his boots and conceal himself in the cart.

Mace's gun roared. A slug tore a bloody welt across Jake's shoulder as Donovan flung himself sideways and down at the last second. Pain seared his shoulder and hot blood flowed, but he knew he had been extremely lucky; it was merely a flesh wound. He knew also if he made another stupid mistake his luck would run out.

Jake turned his lunge into a tumble, which did nothing for the pain lancing his shoulder, that took him five feet to the left. He came up on one knee and jerked a hastily aimed shot towards the now exposed Culverin. The shot missed, splintering wagon wood.

The outlaw fired back. One shot. The hardcase hadn't corrected his aim completely before triggering; that mistake saved

Jake's life. Lead spanged into the ground directly in front of him.

Jake squeezed off two more shots; the first tore through Mace's left arm, the second took him square in the chest, flinging him backward out of the wagon. His ragdoll body thudded in the dirt just beyond the cart and Jake hesitated only a second before gaining his feet and cautiously manoeuvring towards the man's motionless form. He wasn't about to take any chances this time.

His caution proved wasted, however. The brother was dead. This was one time Jake didn't feel any sense of loss.

A shot gathered his attention, sounding from the direction Joe Squatting Rock had taken. Jake wasted no time in heading there.

Joe Squatting Rock felt a raw fire blaze in his gut, the fire of revenge. Long sadness-filled years had he waited to get a chance at Luke Culverin. He vowed the man would die for taking his wife and daughter from him. Joe felt a welt of sorrow lash across his heart. He pushed the pain away. He couldn't let himself feel anything, now. He had to remain dead inside. There would be time for sadness later. He needed all his sharpness for Luke Culverin and pain would only dull his edge. If he lost even a fraction of his guile, he knew he would die. He had learned from experience what the outlaw could do.

Joe had seen the hardcase bound around the corner of a building, bolting towards a small clapboard house to the right. He had fired a shot but missed.

Edging around the corner, Joe's gaze darted in every direction, searching for a target. Silence gripped the surroundings, except for the occasional intrusion of a gunshot from Jake or Mace's gun.

Making his way to the house, he saw the door had been kicked open. He prayed the folks who owned it weren't inside, or, if they were, well hidden.

Joe padded along the wall beside the door, pressing himself flat against the boards and peering in.

Nothing.

He didn't like this. He thought the Culverins would be more open and was prepared for that. Perhaps he had lived among the white man for too long; he had to revert to his Indian ways, the way of stealth and guile.

He slid into the house, careful not to expose himself to a clear shot if Luke were lurking in wait.

Going quickly through the foyer, gun poised, he stepped into an open room that served as dining-room and living-room. A large staircase climbed to the second-floor landing, which ran the length of the double room. Nothing stirred and an ugly feeling pulled at Joe's mind. The Culverin was waiting somewhere nearby; he could feel it.

He crossed the double room to the kitchen, stopping there. Although he had made no noise, something else had. A suppressed sound, furtive, hidden. He listened, relying on his senses to locate it. A door stood to the right, leading to the pantry, he guessed. There. The sound had come from behind the door!

His grip tensed on the Colt. He crept over to the door, gun edged out, and jerked it open, stepping sideways at the same time.

He jerked the Colt up, not firing at the last second as the frightened faces of a young man and woman stared up at him from their crouched position on the pantry floor. They had apparently hidden themselves away in the tiny room. He hated to think how close he had just come to shooting. He jerked a finger to his lips, ordering silence.

'My baby...' the woman muttered in a high-pitched whisper, tears streaming down her face. The man had a petrified expression on his features, terror in his eyes.

'What?' Joe asked, blood running cold.

'He said he'd kill my baby!' the woman blurted, crying.

A laugh boomed from the outer room and Joe spun, his moccasin-clad feet carrying him in almost one move across the kitchen. He jammed his body against the wall and paused, waiting.

'Come on, Injun!' he heard a voice taunt from the outer room. 'I got somethin' for ya. You think I didn't recognize you from a few years back? I couldn't never forgit the face of an enemy, redblood!'

Joe felt a chill shudder through his soul. He edged into the outer room, stopping short as his gaze lifted to the landing. What he saw horrified him, gripping him in a spell of frozen terror for the first time since the day he had witnessed his wife and daughter murdered in cold blood by the outlaw poised on the landing. An evil expression twisted the outlaw's face, as he pushed a little girl in front of him as a shield, making her teeter on the railing, ten feet above the floor. The hardcase's fingers were digging deep into the little girl's arm – she couldn't be more than six or seven, Joe guessed, the same age his daughter had been – as he made obvious his threat to send her hurtling to the floor below. One wrong move and Joe knew the outlaw wouldn't hesitate to send the girl to her death. Tears flowed down the child's face and she seemed utterly paralyzed with terror, unable to even cry out.

'I shoulda killed you, then,' said Luke, gun clenched in his free hand. 'I made a mistake letting you live.'

'Let her go,' said Joe, lips barely moving. He fought against the rage of emotion and fear that froze him. It was roughly six feet from where he stood to the landing. If the outlaw flung the girl, Joe didn't know if he could react in time.

'Hey, no problem, Injun,' Luke sneered. 'But then you gotta come git me!'

'Nooo!' Joe yelled, thrusting out an arm. The outlaw laughed and pushed the little girl forward.

She screamed. Her small form teetered on the rail a second, arms windmilling in an effort to retain her balance, but to no avail. She plunged downward!

The bloody scene of Luke Culverin killing his wife and daughter flashed before Joe's eyes. But it was only a flash and he was in motion, snapping free of the spell that had held him. The girl's teetering had given him a moment's respite. In a blur of motion, he bounded across the floor, dropping his Colt and throwing out his arms. The little girl came down, down, down – into Joe's out-thrust forearms. He curled her towards his body with all his strength, cradling her. The force of the falling body nearly tore his arms from their sockets, but he held on, momentum carrying him forward. He went into a roll to break his fall.

He landed flat on his back, the little girl, who was crying and screaming, sitting on his chest. She scrambled off and he lay there a second, the wind knocked from his lungs. Twisting his head, he saw his gun lying a few feet away and forced himself into motion. Grabbing the Colt, he gained his feet.

Thudding footsteps faded from the upper hall and Joe glimpsed Luke Culverin disappearing into a room.

The little girl ran to her mother, who

grabbed her child and darted into the kitchen.

Joe ascended the stairs in three leaps, not looking back. He knew the child was all right. Reaching the hall, he used more caution until he heard a window break. He shot forward, just in time to see the Culverin dropping from a second-storey window. He raced to the window, saw the brother had disappeared in an alley. Joe threw a leg over the sill and let himself drop gently to the ground. The threat to the little girl had roiled his anger and he knew he was being more reckless than he would have been under normal circumstances. But right now he wanted Luke Culverin more than ever. The outlaw would not escape; he would die for Joe's pain, for the horror-filled memory of his family's murders.

A shot boomed and Joe's left leg buckled. He grabbed for the spot where a slug had torn through his thigh. He crumpled, going down hard on his back. His Colt flew to the right, a foot too far away to reach. Agony seared his leg and blood poured from the wound. He gritted his teeth, cursing his foolhardiness.

A shadow crossed the ground in front of him. Joe looked up – into the face of death!

'Well, lookie here, one dead Injun!' said Luke Culverin, smirking and levelling his gun at Joe's face. 'This time, I'm gonna do it right, redskin.'

A shot boomed. Joe fully expected to feel lead plow into his face. Instead, he saw shock crash on to the outlaw's features. The hardcase stood rigid, too rigid, then folded into a heap that hit the ground with a dead thud.

Behind him stood Jeremy Cross, a rifle smoking in his hands. Joe peered at the breed.

'I figured maybe you were right,' Cross said. 'Maybe it is time to stop running from who – from what I am...'

Jake bounded into the alley, finally locating the source of the shot he had heard when a second, deeper report had sounded – a rifle! He saw Jeremy Cross helping Joe to his feet. Blood was flowing from an ugly hole in the Indian's leg. Jake glanced at the dead form of Luke Culverin, then back to Cross.

'He needs medical attention,' Jake said, indicating Joe. 'Will you get him over to the doc?'

Cross nodded.

'What are you going to do?' Joe asked through clenched teeth. 'There's still two more–'

'No,' Cross interjected, shaking his head. 'Loomis is dead over in the alley yonder. Your deputy got him.'

'Abe? Is he...' Jake felt a snake of coldness slither through his belly.

'He's in a bad way ... I already got him to the doc, but...' Cross shook his head again, tightness on his face.

'Thanks for what you've done, Cross,' said Jake, adjusting his opinion of the man. Whatever it was that riled Cross from his indifference, he didn't care; he was just glad it had. Cross nodded.

'Now get going!' said Jake.

'What about you?' asked Cross, getting a bracing arm around Joe's back.

'There's one left and I've an awful feeling in my gut where he is.' Jake spun and ran from the alley. Yes, he knew where Brent Culverin would be; he had known it from the moment the stage had come back carrying Dave Christie's body and the two Culverins had blown in for a frontal attack. He had pushed the thought to the back of his mind because if he let it stay, he would have lost his edge and never come through this. Worry would have brought his death as sure as a Culverin bullet.

Jake made his way towards the Cazador. He edged to the window, feeling his heart thud in his throat. Anger and worry rushed through his blood like hot knives. Peering through the paneless window, his fear was confirmed. Brent Culverin had his gun jammed to Nellie's temple, her body held in front of the outlaw as a human shield. The hardcase had obviously heard all the shooting and had perhaps decided things weren't going his way.

Jake couldn't risk a shot. The gangleader might reflexively pull the trigger and put a bullet through Nellie's brain.

Jake pulled back from the window and slid around the corner of the building. Going to the back, he found a wooden support beam and, after holstering his gun, shimmied up to the second floor overhang. Getting atop the overhang, he eased his way along the sloped boards until he located a window. It was locked and he used the butt of his Peacemaker on it, trying to be as quiet as the situation would allow. He waited, listening for any sign that the gangleader had caught the sound.

Nothing.

Jake let out the breath he was holding.

After unlocking and raising the window, he clambered through. Making his way through a small room and out into the hall, he could see the hardcase in the barroom proper below, still holding Nellie in front of him. Jake wished he could get off a clear shot without risking her life, but he knew it was impossible. He crept down the hall, suddenly stopping as the outlaw's voice rang out.

'Come on down here, Mr Donovan. I know you're up there.' The outlaw spun Nellie around and looked up, catching Jake full in his sight. He gestured with his gun at Jake, urging him to come down. 'And drop your gun and belt right where you are.'

Jake gritted his teeth, but complied, letting his belt drop to the floor, followed by the Peacemaker.

He came down the hall, then descended the stairs, keeping his gaze glued to the outlaw the whole time. Nothing was preventing the hardcase from filling him full of lead. It was pure bravado keeping Jake alive. Jake hoped he could use the outlaw's ego to his advantage.

Jake reached the bottom of the stairs and came towards them, stopping a few feet away.

'Well, you ain't so mighty after all, are ya? I can assume from you comin' here on your own y'all wounded or killed my brothers...'

Jake didn't say a word. The repulsive half-grin widened on Brent's face.

'You're probably wondering why I don't jest kill you on the spot,' said Brent.

'The thought crossed my mind,' said Jake, his mind feverishly trying to figure a way out of the situation without endangering Nellie's life.

'Simple. I want you to suffer for killing my brothers. Just shooting you'd be too easy – oh, you will die, but not before you see your little filly here get her brains blown clear across Texas! Nobody goes against a Culverin and lives to tell about it! Nobody!' Brent's voice rose to a shrill pitch.

A cold gale blew through Jake. He saw the utter viciousness that shone in the outlaw's black-steel eyes. He meant what he said. Jake had no choice but to try a desperate act; either way, Nellie wasn't likely to survive.

'Say goodbye to your sweatheart, Mr–' The outlaw screamed.

Nellie had stamped a boot heel into the hardcase's instep. Jake heard bones break. The leader relaxed, just barely, the arm jammed under Nellie's chin and she sank her teeth into his flesh. Blood flowed and he jerked the arm away.

Nellie dropped to the floor and Jake moved! Donovan leaped forward, seizing his chance.

The gunman recovered quickly, but not fast enough to get off a shot. Brent swung his gun at Jake's head, but Jake thrust his arm under the blow, deflecting it. The Colt crashed down on Jake's grazed shoulder, sending welts of agony down his arm. Despite the pain, he grabbed Brent's arm and wrenched. The Colt flew away, flying across the floor.

Jake struggled with the outlaw. The hardcase was strong, stronger than Jake. His knee knifed up, nailing Jake in the stomach and knocking the wind from his lungs. Jake fought off a surge of nausea and hurled a fist. Knuckles cracked against the Culverin's jaw, but seemed to have little effect. The outlaw fired back with a blow that glanced from Jake's temple, stunning him.

Jake stumbled a step backward and Nellie burst into motion. She dived for the leader's Colt, but Brent Culverin stamped a foot down on her arm. Nellie let out a bleat as the gunman bent, grabbing her arms and hoisting her into the air. He flung her over a table. She crashed onto the floor and lay still, semi-conscious.

Jake's head settled into a soft jumping. He saw the Culverin leader throw Nellie and fury coursed through his veins, clearing his head. He hurled himself at the outlaw but Brent had already spun to face him, an odd-looking weapon in his hand – the Knuckleduster!

Jake tried to correct his plunge and let momentum carry him out of the line of fire, but was only partially successful. The tiny gun spat and a .32 ripped into Jake's arm.

He felt a spike of deep, burning pain, but blocked the agony from his mind.

Brent Culverin readied for another shot.

In the split second interval before the leader aimed and fired, Jake's hand swept to his waist, plucking loose his Bowie knife. He hurled it as Brent Culverin shifted a foot forward. The knife sliced through the air, glinting, landing with a heavy *thuk* in the leader's stomach, just below the ribcage. The outlaw froze, Knuckleduster dropping to the floor. Blood bubbled from his lips and a dullness washed into his black-steel eyes. He fell backward and hit the floor with a resounding crash, sawdust flying up in a cloud.

Jake's breath pounded out in hot searing gasps and for an instant he didn't move. At last he made his way over to the hardcase to make sure he was dead.

It was over. The Culverin Brothers were no more, but Jake felt little sense of victory. He stepped over the fallen outlaw and went to Nellie, who was coming to her feet.

Clutching his wounded arm, Jake stood there in silence as she clung to him, the heaviness of death settling upon his soul.

'It's what he wanted,' said Jake, peering down at the simple cross of boards upon which they had inscribed the name of Abraham Lincoln Hullar. It jutted from the earth of Widow's Creek Cemetery next to another cross bearing the name of Sheriff Foreman. Jake felt a burden of sorrow in his heart as he looked at Joe Squatting Rock and Jeremy Cross.

'He was a good man,' said Cross, looking at the ground. 'He did his duty and helped saved Matadero.'

'At the cost of his life...' said Jake, shaking his head.

'He knew what he was doing, what he was risking,' said Joe. 'As we all did.'

'Yeah, I guess you're right.' Jake turned away and headed back towards his horse. He mounted, Joe following him and doing the same.

Cross held back a moment, then walked up to them. 'What now?' He eyed them both. Jake didn't answer. 'This town owes you a great debt, Donovan. We're – *I'm* askin' you to stay. We need law here, good law, and both of you...'

Jake forced a smile. 'I've been giving that a lot of thought, Cross, believe me. I spent the last fifteen years wondering if I had a purpose in life. Wondering if I was just born to drift forever. But seeing Nellie threatened by Culverin, knowing I might not be able to save her ... well, that told me my purpose.'

'You'll stay?' Cross's eyes were hopeful.

'I'd already decided to.' Jake's smile grew wider. 'Course I can't speak for Joe here.'

The Indian gave what was as close to a smirk as Jake had seen on him. 'I have nowhere else to go, now. Strange thing about revenge, when it's complete, it leaves you empty.'

'Now, if you don't mind,' said Jake, swinging his bay around, 'we have a wedding to go to.'

'Whose?' yelled Cross as Jake and Joe started towards town.

'Mine!' Jake yelled back. They rode off towards the church of Matadero, Jake feeling a sense of peace for the first time in more than fifteen years. He was home, now, and with Nellie as his wife, he was here to stay.

The publishers hope that this book has given you enjoyable reading. Large Print Books are especially designed to be as easy to see and hold as possible. If you wish a complete list of our books please ask at your local library or write directly to:

Dales Large Print Books
Magna House, Long Preston,
Skipton, North Yorkshire.
BD23 4ND